During and after the last w officer in the Intelligence intelligence duties. Since the advertising agency, a farmer radio station and a PR consultant. He now lives in Kent, with his family.

PALOMINO BLONDE

'Fast-moving, splendidly technocratic intercontinental espionage tale . . . you'll love it'
The Times

THE SPECIAL COLLECTION

'Unskippable conspiracy-thriller . . . to be taken in one enjoyable gulp'
The Guardian

THE MAN WITH THE PRESIDENT'S MIND

'Ingenious and frightening . . . so good it must put him into the bestseller class'
Sunday Express

MOSCOW QUADRILLE

'Remarkably credible . . . high rarity in espionage fiction, an original plot'
The Times

THE TWENTIETH DAY OF JANUARY

'High-level espionage writing. Admirably swift, unmistakably adult'
The Times

By the same author

The Only Good German
A Choice of Enemies
Snowball
Palomino Blonde
The Special Collection
The Man with the President's Mind
Moscow Quadrille
The Lantern Network
The Alpha List
The Reaper
Consequence of Fear
The Twentieth Day of January
The Other Side of Silence
The Lonely Margins
Codeword Cromwell
Shadow of Shadows
All Our Tomorrows
Pay Any Price
The Girl from Addis

TED ALLBEURY

The Secret Whispers

PANTHER
Granada Publishing

Panther Books
Granada Publishing Ltd
8 Grafton Street, London W1X 3LA

Published by Panther Books 1982
Reprinted 1983 (twice), 1985

First published in Great Britain by
Granada Publishing 1981

Copyright © Ted Allbeury 1981

ISBN 0-583-13008-9

Printed and bound in Great Britain by
Cox & Wyman Ltd, Reading

Set in Baskerville

To Tom and Ruth
with love

From camp to camp, through the foul womb of night,
The hum of either army stilly sounds,
That the fix'd sentinels almost receive
The secret whispers of each other's watch.

Wm. Shakespeare
King Henry V

Part One

One

Heinz Kurer stood looking out of the window. It was April in Paris, sunshine and trees, and pretty girls. But he'd got to make that dreary trek down to the Pyrenees and over the Spanish border. He enjoyed training the stooges, and briefing them, but the long boring ritual of showing them the route should not, he reckoned, be left to Abwehr majors. Somebody from the Secret Field Police could do that just as well. Maybe better. Major Kurer was in love with Paris, winter and spring, and with several pretty ladies.

He slid his arms into the old tweed jacket, slung his raincoat over his arm, and picked up his leather case from the bed. He swore softly under his breath as he heard the impatient toot from the car in the street below.

As he opened the street door he saw that at least they'd sent the big Citroën. The driver took his bag and put it in the boot of the car with the official black metal box, then closed the rear door as Kurer slid in beside the other passenger.

'Everything satisfactory last night, my friend?' Kurer spoke in fluent French, and his fellow passenger replied in a French that carried echoes of Alsace-Lorraine. Or Elsass-Löthringen as it was called after the Nazis occupied the disputed territory in 1936. It seemed that his passenger had been very satisfied with the arrangements. It was almost a

11

tradition by now for the stooges to be given a night on the town and an obliging girl as their official send-off. But protocol did not require Abwehr officers to accompany their charges on these last-minute jaunts.

It was mid-afternoon when they turned into the courtyard of the hotel in Clermont-Ferrand and Kurer walked down to the river alone. He sat on the bank near the river's edge, his hands clasped around his knees, staring across the water. He wondered if the training and briefing was a waste of time. They had sent seven of them through to England. They had all landed safely, the girl from the Spanish Embassy had confirmed that every time. Two were sending back stuff but it was pretty low-grade. The kind of information that the Luftwaffe recce patrols brought back every day. Their material was accurate but it added nothing to the picture of the British preparations. A couple of new red pins on the order-of-battle maps, but nothing more. Two others had been caught by the British, tried, found guilty and had ended their lives in front of a firing-squad. The Abwehr had received the usual formal notifications through the International Red Cross in Geneva. The three others had never been heard of again. But two out of seven was not a bad success rate when compared with the stooges whom the Sicherheitsdienst landed from U-boats off the Fife coast in Scotland. Five of those had been executed. One had not been heard from and the other was using his radio back to Berlin. The British thought they had 'turned' him but he'd loyally omitted the second check-word from all his signals and the Abwehr signals unit had played along with it to keep him alive. The material the British gave him to transmit was providing an interesting exercise for the evaluation team.

The trouble was, Kurer thought, that the human material itself was so low-grade. Pimps, thieves, black-market operators were their usual recruits. They got caught by the police for some offence, somebody discovered that they had spent time in England and spoke English, so they got the choice

– Buchenwald or a trip to England. It was a miracle that they didn't all give themselves up the moment they landed. Berlin claimed that the training made them confident, but he doubted that. It was more likely the unspoken threat to their nearest and dearest that kept them in line. But this man Richter could well be the exception. He was above average intelligence, not intellectual but reasonably educated. And this time there was going to be no language problem, and his cover-story was that he wanted to join de Gaulle's Free French. With a German father and a French mother he spoke both languages fluently, and they'd done a lot to iron out the accent. And if you were born in Strasbourg you expect to have a bit of an accent. The Gestapo had handed him over to the Abwehr. It seemed that he had paid for a fake medical certificate to avoid his Wehrmacht call-up, and he'd been sent to a hospital for a thorough check-up and had been found to be in perfect health. With the news from the Russian front, there were hundreds of them trying to dodge the column. Richter was just unlucky.

Kurer looked up at the sky. It was a fine evening and it was going to be the same the next day. His eyes went back to the river as a fish rose close to the bank. It was pleasant enough to be sitting on a river bank in the Auvergne on a spring evening, but he would rather have been in Paris. A meal at Maxim's with Chantelle, then back to his apartment in avenue Kleber, some schmaltzy music on the radio while she undressed, and then she would be standing there smiling and naked. He shook his head to banish the vision and stood up slowly, brushing down his trousers. When the bloody war was over he would have to settle down, or at least be more discreet. But until then he was going to take what was going.

As he walked back to the hotel, he went over the evening's training session in his mind. There was no doubt that Richter was trying hard. Asking sensible questions, absorbing

13

everything he was told, slowly and carefully, like a mincer absorbing meat.

After they had eaten a meal together they went up to his room and spent an hour going over Richter's cover story. His cover story was a good one. Well worked out and based largely on actual fact.

They spent another two hours going over the kind of information they wanted him to send back. And one last time they went over all the illustrations in the handbooks showing the uniforms and insignia of the Royal Navy, the RAF and the Army. Richter wasn't too good at recognizing vehicles and guns, but he tried.

They were both asleep before midnight.

They made a late start the next morning but they were in Perpignan just after mid-day.

As they walked in the sunshine across the Place des Loges, Kurer turned left down a side street, and then left again into a narrow, cobbled street. He spoke casually but quietly. 'Don't look now. We'll stop further on. But the butcher's shop is the place they would take you to. I'll show you his photograph tonight. Right at the top of the building you'll see a small window with blue shutters. That's the room they'd keep you in.'

They walked on a short distance then turned, and Richter looked casually at the butcher's shop as they approached it. It was a small narrow-gutted building, paint peeling from the frame of the small shop window and neither customers nor shop assistants in the shop itself.

Kurer and the stooges never stayed in Perpignan itself. They would inevitably be noticed despite their civilian clothes and good French. Perpignan was more Spanish than French, and more Catalan than either. A strange town that looked quite normal, but where a second town seethed under cover of the ancient buildings and streets. A centre for smuggling, intrigue and politics; there were no strangers in

Perpignan. They knew who you were and what you were doing, inside an hour. They made it their business to know. It was an instinct for survival that was part of their history.

They stayed ten kilometres outside Perpignan at the chateau that had been taken over as the HQ of the local Sicherheitsdienst detachment. Kurer went carefully over the routine that escape lines followed to pass over the Pyrenees and then spent an hour going over the several ways that had been devised for passing the messages to the Abwehr contacts at the Spanish Embassy in London, and a final route for desperately urgent material. He handed over the small phial of pills that would send up Richter's blood pressure for medical checks. They didn't do anything startling but they kept the pressure enough above normal to make it unacceptable for any armed service.

Just below the top of the mountains, they lay panting in the shelter of the rocks as the mist swirled around them. It had taken them seven hours to get that far but Kurer had warned him that the smugglers and gypsies who took the British and French along the escape line would do it in five hours. When they recovered Kurer stood up and Richter followed him.

Half an hour later they were at the summit where two white painted stones on each side of the track marked the frontier. They walked on for almost a kilometre, the mist breaking from time to time to let through the light of the moon. It was in one of those breaks that they saw the shadowy outline of a car, and a light flashed twice towards them.

Kurer greeted the man like the old friend that he was. He was an officer from the Abwehr Stelle at Barcelona. The man driving the car was Spanish – the official liaison man with the Falangists.

Richter dozed off a couple of times as the car bumped and rattled along the pot-holed roads, but Kurer shook him.

'Stay awake, my friend, they might ask you about the scenery.'

Richter rubbed his eyes and fought off the growing need to sleep. As they came to a cross-roads the car slowed down and stopped, and Richter saw a dark blue van with the crest of the Spanish police on its side, and the legend, *Todos por la Patria* .

Handcuffs were clamped round his wrists and he was led into the van. Kurer accompanied him and sat on the metal bench opposite.

'Why do we have to do all this, Herr Major?'

'It's all part of the routine, Erich. They could very easily ask you to describe what happened. You need to know all this.'

'How do we know that this is how the escape line works?'

Kurer smiled. 'We've been able to penetrate some of the lines from time to time. We don't always interfere. That way we learn a lot.'

'How?'

'Some of our own people are part of one or two of the lines. A man escaping can be very grateful to his helpers. It can make him only too ready to talk.'

Richter nodded. It gave him a sense of security to know that everything was worked out so meticulously.

The big double gates of Camp Miranda were already open and the guard saluted as the van passed through and wheeled to a stop outside the main office block.

Inside the office the handcuffs were removed and Kurer and Richter were given a meal. Later Richter was introduced to the Camp Commandant who took them for a short walk around the compound. Back in a small private office Kurer handed over Richter's documents and the small bead-like phial of prussic acid that could end his life, if he wished, in less than sixty seconds. It would be sixty seconds of agony but Kurer didn't mention that. He went over the instructions once more of what Richter would say at the British Embassy in Madrid. He would be taken down to Madrid by private car and accompanied to within sight of the embassy building. The Fatherland, he said, the Abwehr, and Major Kurer himself, wished their hero a successful mission. Erich Richter had never 'belonged' to any sort of group before and there were tears in his eyes as he shook Kurer's hand. Kurer thought that that might be a good sign.

Two

Sergeant-Major Phillips sat in the captain's cabin looking over the typewritten crew-list, comparing each name with the loose-leaf Black List. There didn't seem to be any naughty boys among the crew, but just for the hell of it he pointed at a name. It didn't do to clear a crew-list too easily. People could start putting together cleared lists and build up a picture of the kind of people that British security were looking for, or even not looking for. The opposition could play quite a lot of fancy tunes by analysing lists that had gone unchallenged. Apart from these considerations CSM Phillips felt that it kept merchant ships' captains on their toes. He put his finger against the name CARUANA, Juan. An engineer. Captains got very edgy at the thought of an engineer being taken for questioning. It could end up with their ship missing the next convoy sailing.

Phillips spent an hour cross-questioning Caruana, giving an impression of being not entirely satisfied when he eventually released him back to the engine-room.

There were two more typewritten lists. A list of all passengers. There were thirty, most of them going on to Montreal and Quebec. The second list was of passengers wishing to land at Southampton. There were only four names. Two were a double-act coming home the long way from an Ensa show that had toured the Eighth Army in

North Africa. One was described as an official from the Governor of Gibraltar's staff. Their three passports were lying together on the green baize cloth covering the saloon table.

He checked each passport carefully. Page by page. Entry by entry. There was a slip inside each one giving their reasons for returning to the UK. The official from the Governor's office was a girl, and he remembered that he had been asked to give her an automatic clearance. They had only just discovered that she was five months pregnant. The father, a married lieutenant in the Gloucesters. On the Rock, men outnumbered women in a ratio of about forty to one.

The fourth name was Pierre Maurois and all it said against the name was – refugee. CSM Phillips asked the captain to send for the man. As he waited, Phillips lit a cigarette. There was a routine for refugees. Brief and simple. The sorting out was done at the deep-interrogation centre at Wandsworth, and they didn't like Port Security to go beyond the routine.

Maurois was tall and thin, his fair hair unkempt, his face pale, with an apprehensive air. He seemed surprised when Phillips spoke to him in French.

'How old are you, M'sieur Maurois?'

'Twenty-three.'

'And why have you come to England?'

'I want to join de Gaulle, the Free French.'

'Have you any bags or cases?'

'One small bag.'

'Go and get it and then report back to me here.'

Phillips sat drinking a brandy with the Greek captain who was all hospitality and amiability now that he knew he was free to go into Southampton docks on the next tide.

Ten minutes later Phillips was swinging his leg over the ship's side and fishing around with his foot for a rung of the rope ladder that led down to the drifter that would take him and Maurois back to the security office on the dockside.

He stood looking up the side of the big ship as the Frenchman slowly and clumsily made his way down the ladder. It wasn't easy until you got used to it. There was a thirty or forty foot drop. The sailors held out their hands to Maurois each time the big ship plunged down, and eventually they almost peeled him off the ladder to the heaving deck of the drifter.

Phillips phoned the central police station in Southampton and an hour later a Special Branch man came over to pick up the Frenchman and take him up to Wandsworth.

Two days later Captain David Miller, Intelligence Corps, sat at the table, looking over the Frenchman's documents and the lab reports.

Everything was genuine. The Carte d'Identité, the Permis de Conduire, and the birth certificate. There was a brief note from the laboratory to point out that the ink of the signature, and the stamp itself, on the Carte d'Identité seemed fresher than the issue date would indicate. But they emphasized that there seemed to be no question of forgery.

He tucked them all back in the file and sent them to Central Registry. It would be three days before he could start interrogating the Frenchman.

He walked over to French Archives to see if she was there. Captain Miller had an eye for the girls, and the girls weren't averse to him. Female opinion reckoned that there was a touch of Errol Flynn about the captain. But David Miller was gradually coming to the conclusion that if Penny Lucas would have him on a permanent basis he would be prepared to forswear all others. Females were thick on the ground at the interrogation centre for a very good reason. They were more secure than men. They felt no urge to impress their dates with hints about the secret and vital work that occupied their days and nights. This wasn't because they were more patriotic than men but because they saw no glamour in their jobs. They wouldn't have been impressed by similar hints from men. Unfortunately young men never realized that they boasted in vain; and that one red rose would have got them further much quicker.

Penny Lucas wasn't the prettiest girl at the centre. A blonde girl in Jugoslav Archives held that award, but Penny was a strong contender, and pretty enough to have had a film contract with Rank before she was called up to the services. She spoke good French and the Army had been in two minds about where she should go. It would be either SOE or the Royal Victoria Patriotic School at Wandsworth, the deep-interrogation centre. Her French wasn't quite good enough for SOE field work, and as the RVPS was clamouring for assistants that was where she had been posted.

Like most girls serving the more secret sections of British intelligence, she came from a good family. Her father had been born in Paris, the only son of a banking family. Despite parental pressure he had come to London in his teens to study at the Slade. By his early twenties he was a portrait artist in a small way, and when he was twenty-seven he had become a naturalized Britisher. It was a condition laid down by his fiancée's parents if they were to marry. His own parents took it as the insult it was, but the young man himself was only amused. He was a man who disliked any kind of conflict.

Penny's parents had met David Miller a number of times. Her mother disliked him intensely. But that was par for the course. Mrs Lucas disliked all her daughter's boyfriends. She was a plump, petulant woman who dominated the whole household from her comfortable armchair. Her weapon was her heart. An organ that defied medical diagnosis but allowed her to impose her will on those around her.

David Miller was sometimes puzzled by Penny's attitude when they were at her home. He guessed that she knew well enough that her mother's heart was virtually as strong as her own, but she became a small girl again, controlled and dominated by remote control from the armchair, going out of her way to avoid sitting with him, listening silently as her mother tried to dominate him too. She even reproved him sometimes when her mother went too far and he amiably resisted her domineering attitude.

If they had not been mother and daughter he would have suspected them of having some sort of passive lesbian relationship. The older woman's possessiveness and domination were unpleasant enough, but her daughter's willingness to change her whole personality in front of her mother struck him as either juvenile or sick. He wasn't sure which. He didn't dwell on it, but he was aware that her mother was an avowed enemy.

Penny's education had ended at Roedean. The screen test and the subsequent contract had got in the way of university. There hadn't been a film. Four months at the Rank charm school had made her call-up a welcome relief. She had neat, even features, and a nice young body, but it was her big brown eyes that pole-axed Captain Miller. There were times, when his hands were moving into forbidden territory when those two brown eyes seemed able to hypnotize him into inaction.

She had several boyfriends, but like Easter, they were movable feasts, and they generally got posted before long to some far-flung outpost of the Empire. She was very fond of David. He was good-looking, lively and intelligent, but she thought that he was also a bit too self-contained. Despite the amiable exterior there was a ruthlessness underneath that boded ill for those who crossed him. Maybe it was because of the war and what he was doing. She was in no hurry. There was plenty of time to find out what he was really like. All she knew of his background was that he had been brought up in an orphanage.

She turned to look at him. 'I'm not going to make it by seven, Dave.'

'When?'

'More like eight.'

'Can I help?'

'No. It's a ferreting job. Somebody's filed the Paris Gestapo records in the wrong place. It's just a process of elimination.'

He looked at his watch. 'I'll start on the Frenchman then, and get the preliminaries over. I'll be in 107, give me a knock when you're ready.'

'OK.'

Miller looked across at the Frenchman. He looked uneasy, but most of them did, innocent or guilty; being interrogated was an ordeal. It was meant to be an ordeal. He pressed the button on the leg of the table and waited for the red light to come on over the door. When it flickered, and then held, he knew that the wire-recorder was working. He looked across the table and leaned back in his chair to give an air of relaxation.

'Your name?'

'Pierre Maurois.'

'Date of birth?'

'March first, 1918.'

'Place of birth?'

'Paris.'

'Father's nationality?'

'French.'

'Mother's?'

'French.'

'What was your work when you left?'

'I was a clerk.'

'Where?'

'At Renault.'

'What department?'

'I was a progress clerk.'

'Go on.'

'I was responsible for checking on tank tracks from the foundry to assembly.'

'What made you decide to come to England?'

'I listened to de Gaulle on the BBC.'

'Why weren't you called up for the French Army before the occupation?'

'I was in a reserved occupation.'

'You could have volunteered.'

'That wasn't allowed without permission from the Ministry of Labour. I wasn't all that keen in those days anyway.'

'What contacts have you had with the German authorities?'

'Only the two Germans in charge of production at Renault.'

'Have you had any contact with resistance groups in France?'

'No.'

'Do you belong to any political party?'

'No.'

'A trades union?'

'Yes.'

'Which one?'

'CGT.'

The Frenchman turned as he heard the knock on the door but Miller ignored it.

'Have you had a meal?'

'Yes.'

'Cigarettes?'

'I don't smoke.'

Miller stood up, pressed the bell twice and waited for the Field Security sergeant to take the Frenchman away.

Penny was waiting for him in the corridor.

Three

Despite the fact that it was the middle of June the interrogation cell was cold, and the smell of fresh whitewash on the cement walls gave a stale dampness to the air.

The transcript of the previous short interrogation was in the file on the table and as Miller lit a cigarette, he said, 'Will it worry you if I smoke?'

Maurois shook his head. 'Not at all.'

'Tell me about your journey.'

'I found a man in Perpignan who took me over the frontier.'

'Let's go back before that. How did you travel to Perpignan?'

'By train.'

'From what station?'

'Gare d'Austerlitz.'

'What time did it leave?'

'I can't remember.'

'Morning, afternoon, or night?'

'I think it was afternoon.'

'Where did the train stop?'

'I don't remember. I slept most of the time.'

'You weren't scared there would be a security check?'

'Not really.'

Miller noted the hesitation. 'You don't remember any stops on the way?'

'I think we stopped at Pau.'

'Are you sure?'

'Yes. I'm sure we did.'

'We?'

Maurois shrugged. 'The passengers.'

'What time did you arrive in Perpignan?'

'In the evening.'

'What time?'

'I don't remember.'

'Was it dark?'

'Just about.'

'Where did you stay?'

'At an inn.'

'Name?'

'Flêche d'Or.'

'Go on.'

'A man approached me next day and asked if I wanted to go over the frontier. He said he could arrange it.'

'How much did he want?'

'Twenty thousand francs.'

'And you accepted?'

'Yes.'

'Go on.'

'He took me to a butcher's shop. I stayed there one night and he took me over the next day.'

'Was it an easy journey?'

Maurois shrugged. 'I suppose so. He was all right but I was done in.'

'Did you stop on the way?'

'We stopped just short of the top.'

'What happened?'

Maurois looked surprised. 'Nothing. We just rested and then went on.'

'Carry on.'

'He left me at the border and about two kilometres inside I was picked up by Spanish police and put in a van.'

'Yes?'

'They took me to a prison.'

'Where?'

'I don't know. It was called Miranda.'

'What happened?'

'They said I was part of a Catalan terror group and put me in a cell. They kept me there for three days and then they released me.'

'Were you in a solitary cell?'

'Yes.'

'Do you remember the number?'

'No.'

'What could you see from the window?'

'I don't think there was a window. I don't remember.'

'Describe the butcher's shop for me.'

'What butcher's shop?'

'The one in Perpignan.'

'Oh. It was in a cobbled street. I was in a room at the top with blue shutters.'

'What was the patron like?'

'A fat man. Round face. Bald.'

'What colour eyes had he got?'

'Blue, I think.'

'What happened after you left Miranda?'

'I went to the Embassy at Madrid and they made arrangements for me to go to Gibraltar and catch the boat.'

He spent another two hours going back over the questions again and again, slipping in an extra question here and there, extending an answer, tying down hours and minutes. He already knew the man was a phoney but he wanted to sort out the best way to break him down. He was probably another one of Kurer's men. The Germans never seemed to learn. Once they'd worked out what seemed to them a good routine, they stuck to it no matter what. They had already been notified of at least four failures through the Red Cross. Maybe they thought it was a ploy by the British. But they must know that nothing was going through to them.

He looked across at Maurois. 'We'll take a break this afternoon and I'll talk to you again some time tomorrow.'

'Is it going to be all right?'

'Is what going to be all right?'

'All this. Me.'

Miller leaned back, looking at Maurois, whistling through his teeth, trying to remember the words of 'Dearly Beloved'.

'What do *you* think, my friend?'

Maurois pursed his lips. 'I just hope. That is all.'

'That's all any of us can do,' Miller said, smiling, as he stood up.

Miller walked slowly down the narrow passage, out of the door and across to the other wing. He showed his pass to the guard who let him go through to the building.

The woman at the desk was in her late forties. A handsome woman with shrewd but tired eyes. The wife of a judge, she was responsible for the administration of the evaluation section. She played no part in the actual evaluations but she was a buffer between impatient, demanding interrogation officers, the reference section, and the evaluation section itself. Mrs Selwyn-Frazer was tough but diplomatic.

'Well, Captain Miller, what can we do for you?'

'There's about three hours of recording from 107. I was wondering when I could get the report.'

Mrs Selwyn-Frazer looked at her gold watch.

'Not today I'm afraid.'

'Tomorrow morning?'

'Is it straightforward?'

'Pretty well.'

'Let's say 14.00 hours tomorrow. On the dot.'

'Can you send it through to me?'

'Of course.'

'Any news of Sammy?'

'Just the official notification from Geneva. He's in a PW hospital in Italy somewhere. No other details. Joe's pulling strings like mad to find out more. All we can do is hope.'

Miller felt that everybody was doing a lot of hoping that day.

Evaluation Report	F/R/10741
Interrogation Room	107
Interrogation Officer	Miller D. Capt. Int. Corps.
Date Interrogation	4th and 7th June 1943
Recording duration	1 – 23 mins. 4 secs.
	2 – 97 mins. 00 secs.
Evaluation officer	Sykes M.R. Lieut. FANY
Evaluation report date	8th June 1943
Detainee's name	MAUROIS, Pierre

1. All trains PARIS – PERPIGNAN terminated NARBONNE second and third weeks April. Buses onwards to PERPIGNAN. Line disrupted by sabotage. No railway traffic as far as PAU. (See file SOE 19046.)

2. Sabotage of railway lines also confirmed by the usual rise in price of oranges on Paris market owing to shortage of supplies from the South.

3. Butcher's shop PERPIGNAN not used by escape lines since first week March.

4. No second demand for extra payment by guide prior to crossing frontier.

5. All cells at CAMP MIRANDA have barred windows. (See model in archive section.)

6. Voice pattern gives no indications beyond normal nervousness.

7. Speech analysis indicates timbre and accent of Alsace-Lorraine area. Distinct indications of German 'L'.

SUMMARY.

This detainee has all standard indications of Abwehr 'plant'. Suggest further interrogation on those lines.

Final laboratory report MAUROIS, Pierre. Dated 7.6.43
Carte d'Identité and Permis de Conduire.

Signatures and stamps on both documents appear to be genuine but in both cases are incompatible with date of issue. Date of issue is given as Jan.6.1943 but ink analysis of signature much later. Same applies to ink of stamp. This incompatibility has been noted before on documents issued by Abwehr Stelle Paris for line-crossers. We assume that blank documents are signed and stamped in batches to be used later as required, hence discrepancy. See RVPS files 407/14, 503/7, 609/9, 707/2 and 1012/7.

Four

Maurois was watching Miller's face for some indication of his attitude.

'Did you sleep well, M'sieur Maurois?'

'Not too bad.'

Miller leaned forward, his elbows on the table, looking directly at Maurois. 'We've got a problem, I'm afraid.'

'What's that?'

Miller was silent for a moment and then he said softly, 'When did you last see Major Kurer?'

He saw the shock on the man's face, and the sudden fear in his eyes. He thought it must be like that when the bullfighter sticks his sword in for the kill. The moment of truth when the world seems to stop and fear floods in. Maurois swallowed, and tried to pull himself together.

'I don't know who you mean.'

'He's an Abwehr officer. A good-looking man about thirty years old. He trains the line-crossers and then takes them down to Perpignan and over the frontier. A clever man, but very careless. Likes the girls. When did you last see him?'

'I don't understand.'

'You do, my friend. You may not like it, but you understand. Kurer's dropped you in the shit. Just like he did all the others.'

'What others?'

'The other line-crossers. Seven or eight so far. No doubt there'll be more to come.'

'The Geneva Convention.'

'What about it?'

'I claim its protection.'

Miller laughed. 'Is that what he told you to do? He's a naughty fellow is Kurer. The Geneva Convention only covers prisoners of war, soldiers, sailors and airmen. You're a spy, my boy, an agent in civilian clothes.'

Maurois sat silent, shivering, his eyes closed, his arms folded round his chest as if he was holding himself together.

'You've been very stupid, mister,' Miller said softly.

Maurois looked up slowly and Miller knew that he was trying to decide whether to go on bluffing or call it a day.

'I'll try and help you, Pierre, if you stop playing games.'

'How can you help me?'

'I can tell the court that you co-operated.'

'What will the court do?'

'I don't know. All the others have co-operated fully and they didn't go to court.'

'What happened to them?'

'They're all right. They're still alive.'

'Prisoners?'

'Don't worry about *them*, my friend. Worry about yourself.'

'What happens if I co-operate?'

'It depends on how far you go.'

Maurois shook his head and shrugged. 'I don't know about these situations.'

'You're German aren't you? What's your real name?'

'Richter. Erich Richter.'

'And you come from Alsace?'

'My God. How do you know that?'

'Where were you born?'

'Strasbourg.'

32

'Why did Kurer want you to join the Free French?'

'He didn't. I've got pills to raise my blood pressure for medicals. He said I would be rejected and be given a civilian job. Joining the Free French was just a cover.'

'Would you rather talk in German?'

'It's all the same to me.'

'Have you ever been in prison?'

'No.'

'How did they recruit you?'

'I was picked up by the Gestapo for avoiding call-up. They gave me the choice. Jail, or this business.'

'You'd have done better to have chosen jail.'

The man sighed and shrugged. 'It's too late.'

'Are you married?'

'No.'

'Any dependants?'

'No.'

'Do you speak any English?'

'No. But I could learn.'

'What were you supposed to report on?'

'Troop positions and movement of troops.'

'How were you to send the stuff back?'

'Through the Spanish Embassy.'

Miller smiled. 'Lemon juice and Señora Ramirez?'

'Yes.'

'And the history shelf at Holborn Library for emergencies?'

Richter shook his head in disbelief. 'You know as much as me, m'sieur.'

'More, I expect.' Miller stood up. 'I'll see you again tomorrow.'

'What will happen to me?'

'I don't know. I'll have to think about it. You think about it too.'

Miller telephoned the GII I(b) at the War Office who liaised with the committee. He didn't think his committee would be interested. They already had several 'turned' German agents with radio sets operating back to both the Abwehr and the SD, and the laborious communications through the Spanish Embassy wouldn't be likely to interest them.

But he'd been fetched out of the local flea-pit at ten o'clock that evening, where he'd taken Penny to see Bing in *Holiday Inn*. He was to phone the GII I(b) immediately. Neither of them could have guessed that that telephone call was going to echo down their lives long after they had forgotten about it.

He got his statutory good-night kiss, and found once again that a pocket, a uniform jacket, a khaki shirt, and an Army issue bra, still provided excellent protection for young women's bosoms.

The duty officer was playing out some classic chess game on his pocket chess-set and waved a magnanimous hand towards the phone.

The GII I(b) was traced to his club. The committee were very interested in Miller's minnow, and he was to report to Room 241 at the War Office at 11.00 hours the following morning. Barathea, not battle-dress, would be worn, it seemed.

There had been two full colonels at the meeting, and the GII, an elderly major. They were very interested in Richter, and Miller was to check out his background. Social and political. There was no great hurry, but they wanted a weekly report and expected that a month should be sufficient. They wouldn't give any hint of what they were looking for or even what they wanted to avoid. He should go in without prejudice, and establish as close a relationship as he deemed necessary. He could take Richter outside the interrogation centre but he was to be back every night. Not even the vaguest hint would be given that anyone was interested in him.

*

For the first few days, Miller walked in the grounds at Wandsworth with Richter. He found him a few books in German, and talked casually about Richter's childhood and family background, fending off questions about what was going to happen to him.

On the first Saturday he had taken Richter to Lord's cricket ground to watch the Army XI play the RAF XI, and in the evening they had gone to the cinema to see *For Whom the Bell Tolls*. Slowly, over the next few days, Richter relaxed, no longer asking compulsive questions about courts and sentences.

When Miller sent in his report at the end of the second week he was called to London for a meeting the next day. This time the meeting was in one of the Regency houses in a square at the back of Selfridges. And this time it was just one of the colonels. No bright red insignia of the General Staff, but a light grey pair of Daks and a Harris tweed jacket. Colonel Mayne looked, and talked, as if he were the permanent understudy for C. Aubrey Smith. He poured them each a whisky and then, leaning his head confidentially towards Miller, said, 'Tell me what you make of him – an all-round impression.'

'He comes from a working class family. Father German, a welder, a strong trades-unionist, and his mother was French. Lower middle-class. Both his parents were born in Metz. Richter himself was born in Strasbourg. Not much education but a shrewd quick mind. He would have learned quickly if he'd ever had the chance.'

Mayne turned to look at him. 'A chip on his shoulder about all this?'

'Well aware of the unfairness, but no chip. He sees his opportunities to come some time in the future.'

'Politics?'

'Social-democrat thinking, but nothing in any formal way.'

'A commie d'ye reckon?'

'No. Could be converted perhaps.'

'A member of the Nazi party?'

'No. I doubt if they'd have him anyway.'

'Why not?'

'He's mentally tough but not physically tough. And he's no fanatic about anything.'

'Scared at the moment?'

'Very scared at first, but he's got it under control now.'

'Would he co-operate with you if you gave him the chance?'

'I'm sure he would.'

'How would you go about it?'

'Depends on what it was.'

One watery blue eye looked at him speculatively.

'Are you fishing, young man?'

'Yes, sir.'

'We want to use him. Part of a bigger scheme. But he would be important. And if he double-crossed us there'd be hell to pay. Lives lost. Heads would roll. Mine as well as yours. Would you trust him?'

'No, sir.'

The white eye-brows went up.

'Why not?'

'I'd never let a turned man get in a position where I had to trust him. I should fence him round. Scare him.'

'Glad to hear that. How long do you want to break him in?'

'About a week.'

'Any help you want?'

'What's he going to do?'

'He's going to do exactly what they told him to do, but we're going to tell him what to say.'

'It's a pretty crude system they provide for these chaps.'

'It'll suit us, captain. It'll suit us.'

As Colonel Mayne stood up he looked at his watch.

'You hungry? D'you want to have a meal?'

'No, thank you, sir.'

Five

For the first time in over two weeks Richter was escorted formally to the interrogation cell. And for the first time ever Miller was not already there, waiting for him.

He sat down on his usual side of the heavy oak table and the Field Security corporal stood at the door, the flap on his canvas holster open to show the wooden butt of his Smith and Wesson.

Richter began to shift about uneasily when Miller had not appeared after fifteen minutes. He turned to look at the corporal. 'Does the captain know I'm here?'

'Shut up, you German bastard.'

He saw the anger in the corporal's eyes and all his self-confidence evaporated. As the minutes went by, he thought that perhaps the corporal was an exception. A German-hater, and too unimportant to know that he had certain privileges.

Then Miller came in, dismissing the corporal. He neither greeted nor looked at Richter, but settled himself carefully in his chair before he looked across the table. His face solemn, his eyes watchful. 'I'm afraid I've got bad news, Erich.'

'What is it?'

'The authorities are insisting that you go before a court.'

'But I've co-operated.'

Miller's head came up quickly. 'How do you mean?'

'I've told you how they sent me over and what I had to do.'

'Unfortunately the courts would claim that we already knew all that, and that you merely confirmed what we knew.'

'What more can I do for God's sake?'

'I don't know. Would you volunteer to work in a factory if that would help?'

'Yes. Of course I would.'

'I'm sorry about this, Erich. I'd hoped that they would accept my recommendation. You'll be given a lawyer of course but I think they want to make an example of you. They want to teach the Abwehr a lesson.'

'What does that mean?'

'A public trial as a spy. The world press there.'

'Jesus. They'd crucify me.'

'I know. That's what I'm afraid of. We've got to think up something between us. Something that could make them think again.' Miller stood up. 'Let's take a walk in the grounds. We won't be able to do that after today.'

Richter shivered as they walked in the hot sun, even more agitated than he had been when Miller had first exposed him. Miller knew how he felt. He had laid on the scenario in the interrogation room to lower Richter's morale. The terrible deflation that would get worse during the night. After fifteen minutes he escorted Richter back to the guard-room and booked him in.

Penny was looking towards the pond where small boys were sailing their model boats, a stalk of grass between her strong white teeth. She took the green stalk from her mouth and turned to look at him. 'What's going on with you and your kraut, David?'

'Just interrogating him.'

38

'I thought you'd finished all that. I heard you'd made him spill the beans.'

His grey eyes looked at her. 'Did you now?'

She smiled. 'Are you doing your strong, silent man bit?'

'No. And I'm not going to ask you how many lost files there are in Archives either.'

She laughed. 'The answer's none, my boy, at this moment. We've been having a blitz.'

Her small hand was on the grass beside her, and his hand gently closed over it.

'Will you marry me, Penny?'

She smiled. 'But I don't meet your specification.'

'What the hell's that?'

'Tony Martin told one of the girls that you had once announced in the mess that the only girl you'd ever consider marrying was a beautiful blonde, with long legs, big tits, and a large private income.'

'Lieutenant Martin is a drunken, lying bum.'

She was grinning. 'It sounds terribly *like* you.'

'Thanks for the compliment.'

'*Did* you say that?'

'I'm afraid so.'

And they both burst out laughing. Then she said, 'I've got long legs but ... '

'Shut up. It was a joke, in bad taste. I expect you and your girlfriends say the same kind of things when you're having one of your jolly hockey-sticks sessions. But you're all too crafty to tell tales.'

'You're very touchy tonight, my boy.'

'So maybe you'd like to answer my question.'

'Do you want to sleep with me?'

'Of course I do.'

'You don't have to marry me to do that.'

He stood up, reaching for her hand to pull her up. As she stood up she was very close to him and her eyes were smiling

39

at him. 'Captain David Miller, Intelligence Corps, knight in shining armour. Yes, I'll marry you.'

And as they stood there beside the pond at Clapham Common, kissing passionately, the small boys forgot their boats and watched in silence. Couples on Clapham Common provided a lot of entertainment for small boys. But this couple was a wash-out, they just walked away hand in hand. The consensus was that sailors were much better value than soldiers.

The next morning Miller took Richter to Hyde Park. They had hardly spoken on their walk but as soon as they were seated by the pond in Kensington Gardens Richter turned to him. 'Is there anything more I could tell you? Things that you don't know.'

'We've got all we need to know about the Abwehr Stelle in Paris. D'you know anything about the Stelle in Hamburg?'

'No. Nothing.'

'Maybe there's something we could think of for you to do.'

'I'd do anything you asked.'

Miller looked at Richter's face as if he were searching for some answer, some solution.

'How about ... ' he said slowly as if he were just forming the thought, '... how about you offer to help us by pretending to do your job for the Abwehr?'

'How could I do that?'

'You could send messages back to them as if you hadn't been caught.'

'I'd have nothing to report.'

'We could give you the messages to send.'

'They'd soon realize that the information was fake. They've got other sources they could use for checking on my stuff.'

'What we gave you would be true. Actual facts.'

'Do other prisoners do that?'

'You wouldn't be a prisoner, Erich,' Miller said, avoiding the question. 'You'd be a collaborator.'

Richter sighed. 'And when the Wehrmacht come over here they'd hang me. If I was lucky.'

'Erich, the war's over for the Nazis. It's just a matter of time. Once they invaded Russia they were half-finished. When the United States came in, that was the end for the Third Reich.'

'And if I did this, would the court take a different view?'

'You wouldn't even go to court. Your status would have changed. They would have no jurisdiction over you. Not unless you did something stupid.'

'Can you arrange this?'

'I'll try to. I'll talk to them as soon as I get back. Do you want to think it over first?'

'No. I just want to get out of this mess.'

'How do you feel about doing this?'

'I'll feel like a traitor. I shall *be* a traitor.'

'You'll be saving lives, Erich. German lives as well as Allied lives. They're madmen. The Nazis are dragging Germany deep into the mud. The Nazis never did anything for you. They forced you to do this.'

'That's true.' Richter nodded, as if for the first time he was convinced of the rightness of what he was doing. Miller knew that like all the others he wanted a face-saver, and when Miller laid them out for him to choose he had picked the one he fancied most.

On 25 July David Miller married Penelope Hope Lucas in the parish church at Limpsfield, Surrey. A distant Miller cousin played the organ. The hymn was 'The voice that breathed o'er Eden', chosen by the bride's father. Unfortunately Mrs Lucas's heart condition prevented her from attending the wedding. They walked back down the aisle together, arms linked, beaming happily to the resounding chords of Elgar's Nimrod variation from the Enigma Suite, chosen by the groom himself. It was a real bride's day with hot sun, and cow-parsley and poppies standing high along the hedges.

They had been given two days leave which they spent at the Savoy. In Italy that day, the population celebrated the fall of Mussolini.

Richter sat reading the text of the message that had been provided for him to copy out. He turned to look at Miller who was smiling. 'Why are you smiling?'

'Where did Kurer suggest you got the lemon juice?'

'From a lemon.'

'And where would you get a lemon?'

'From a shop.'

'There haven't been lemons in the shops here for nearly two years.'

'There are lemons in Germany.'

'Sure, but they come from Italy by land. We don't risk sailors' lives for lemons.'

'They won't realize that.'

'There's a lot they don't realize. Have you written out the cover letter?'

'Yes.'

Miller read through the innocuous letter, checked it against the typewritten copy and then handed it back. He pushed across the egg-cup half-filled with lemon juice and the pen.

'You've got to make it word for word.'

'OK.'

'You're sure you were only given the one check-word?'

'Quite sure.'

Miller sat watching as Richter wrote out the invisible message between the lines. The message that had been put together by the special team who provided the carefully chosen material for 'turned' agents.

When Richter had finished, Miller took the letter, and holding it carefully, he walked out of the room and down the corridor. The duty officer in the laboratory was waiting for him. He placed the paper on top of several sheets of blotting paper then lifted a domestic electric iron, checked its heat near his cheek and placed it lightly on the paper, smoothing it slowly and carefully over the whole surface. He waited for the paper to cool and then ironed it again.

Miller looked it over carefully. In places the brown writing between the lines was hard to decipher, but it was word for word what Richter had been given to write. Commas, full-stops, all correct, and no additional marks of any kind.

Now that they'd checked that he wasn't playing games, Richter could write the letter and the hidden message again. It did no harm to let him know that he was under constant surveillance.

He stood in the telephone kiosk with Miller as he spoke to the girl in the Spanish Embassy. He gave her the code-word and she replied with one word. A number.

The number was three, and nominated the dead-letter drop where the letter was to be placed. The drop was under the window-box of a basement flat in Pont Street. A Special Branch officer confirmed the next morning that the letter had been picked up by a man from the embassy's Central Registry at 11.10 pm.

A further message was sent by Richter three weeks later. The team decided that no further messages would go until there had been a response. Miller was instructed to do nothing, but to accompany Richter wherever he wanted to go until he was returned to his cell each night.

The small tobacconist and newsagent's shop in Great Newport Street had a glass case alongside its entrance door. The case held twenty or so postcards offering the services of prostitutes in the coy code that the law required. Young models with big Italian chests offered them for sale, young women eagerly sought gentlemen who wanted to be corrected, and it seemed that a number of young lovelies had friendly cats for sale. There was a rather fly-blown card offering painting and decorating services, and two weeks after Richter had sent the second message there was a plain white card offering a second-hand copy of André Maurois' *Les Silences du Colonel Bramble* for two pounds three shillings. A telephone number was given, and when Richter called the number he was given the address of a hotel in Paddington.

The hotel was a sleazy boarding house in Sussex Gardens. The front door was open and Richter's letter was lying on the hall table with half a dozen others, just as he had been told on the telephone. Nobody checked him, and he slid the letter into his jacket pocket and walked out.

The two of them walked to a small café and Richter handed the letter to Miller, who slid it into his inside pocket. They drank their coffees and left, catching the bus back to Wandsworth where Miller passed the letter to forensic.

The laboratory identified the finger-prints of Richter and Miller, and there were prints and part-prints of half a dozen others. The message itself was typewritten and they checked it letter by letter under a microscope. There were no micro-dots, and no irregularities. It had been typed in a standard typeface on a French typewriter.

The message itself was not in code but merely made oblique references so that a casual reader might find it innocuous. It was signed with the single letter K. It was in French. It implied a cautious approval.

Dear Friend,
    Received your welcome letter. What is your new job? All here well satisfied with present situation.
    Would like to know more about the second group of friends that you saw. What else did they tell you apart

from the story of the jumping pig? Sounds all very amusing. There are no doubt other stories they tell equally interesting. How many were there at that place and have they got other homes? Are they working hard? Let us know what they are doing. Do they have transport of any kind?

Write me again soon.

K.

The jumping pig obviously referred to the 30 Corps' corps sign of a leaping wild boar, and they wanted him to identify the divisional signs and support group signs. They wanted to know where the various units were located and the types of their transport. It matched the information they had sent through to Kurer. They would already have a fair knowledge of 30 Corps' battle-order and they were merely checking out Richter's accuracy and his ability to check more specific details. And they were testing out whether he had been 'turned'.

Six

With permission granted for them to live out, David and Penny Miller had found two rooms with kitchen and bathroom, ten minutes walk from the RVPD. And it was there, on a Sunday evening, that they had their first quarrel.

They had just finished their meal, and Penny had brought in the coffee. As she sat down she said, 'What's going on with Richter?'

She actually didn't give a damn what was 'going on' with Richter. She was merely intending to show a passing interest in her husband's work. She looked up, surprised, when he said, 'Who's Richter?'

'Your kraut. The line-crosser.'

She frowned as she saw the cold, hard eyes of her husband across the table.

'What's the matter, Dave?'

He shifted in his chair and then leaned forward with his elbows on the table. 'Maybe we'd better get something straight, sweetie. I don't ask you questions about your work, and you don't ask me questions about mine. OK?'

'For God's sake, I'm your wife. Remember?'

'What's that got to do with it?'

'Wives and husbands don't have secrets from one another.'

46

'I've got news for you, Penny. This husband and wife do have secrets from one another. They've both signed a piece of paper to that effect.'

'Oh, rubbish. That means other people. Outsiders. We work in the same place for heaven's sake.'

'All the more reason why we should stick to the rules.'

She put her head on one side as she looked at him. 'You know, sometimes I think I don't know much about you. Right now you seem like a stranger.'

He smiled. 'How about going to bed with a stranger. Could be fun.'

She shrugged. 'Mary and Peter are coming in for a drink.'

'They won't be here for twenty minutes at least.'

She stood up. 'I've got things to do.'

He made no move to heal the breach and he had been conscious of her aloofness while they were chatting with their friends.

When they were alone he poured them both a last drink, and raising his glass to her, grinning, he said, '*Prosit*, Mata Hari.'

The wine was warm when it hit his face, and the big wet stain on his white shirt looked like blood. He wiped his mouth with the back of his hand and then looked across at her.

He said quietly, 'If you were a man I'd knock your front teeth out. As you're a woman I'll just say that you've got the makings of a shrew. And as you're my wife I'll say only this. Don't ask me about my work. People's lives depend on me not talking. And if ever you put on another performance like tonight I'll walk out and I won't be back. I love you. I like being married to you. But my work is a separate thing. If this bloody war ever ends I'll tell you almost anything you want to know.'

She sat looking at him in long moments of silence. Then she said, 'I was stupid, Dave. I didn't really want to know.

47

I was just chatting. It just went on because I felt as if you were closing me out. I'm sorry.'

He smiled. 'Forget it, kid.' And he reached across for her hand.

By the end of the year Richter was given two rooms at the RVPS and a reasonable amount of freedom. So long as he was escorted he could go wherever he liked in the London area.

The traffic with the Abwehr continued, and the replies from Paris. And the kind of information they asked for indicated that he was not only trusted but seen as a key agent.

In February 1944, the control team started their planned deception to protect Operation Overlord. A similar operation using 'turned' radio-operators was mounted against the Wehrmacht's special unit, Fremde Heere West, which was responsible for building up the order of battle of the Allied forces.

The Abwehr Stelle in Paris had been pressing Richter to attempt to get into the Defence Zone on the south coast. Gold sovereigns had been passed through to him via the Spanish Embassy. His 'cover story' to the Abwehr was that he was working as a salesman for an electrical contractor which was why he was able to travel around the country without problems. The main thrust of the deception was to confuse the German High Command as to where the actual D-day landings would be.

The rivalry between the various German intelligence services had existed before the war, but had intensified during the war years. By March, 1944, the Abwehr was being attacked by Himmler as inefficient and of doubtful loyalty. The information from their agents was suspect. But all information on the time and place of the Allied landings was now top priority.

When it became clear that Adolf Hitler was beginning to

doubt even the possibility of an Allied invasion, and alternatively, that if it came it would be no more than a large local battle, the Wehrmacht gritted its teeth and made plans of their own to convince him otherwise.

The Wehrmacht's sophisticated team at Fremde Heere West began to create non-existent British and US military units amounting to 30 divisions. The Allies themselves had created 'phantom' divisions and brigades that were no more than special signals units putting out spurious signals traffic as deception. Foreign Armies West had been only partially deceived, but under pressure from the Generals they now accepted as real what they knew not to be. At least it stopped Hitler from pulling out units for the East front that would be vital for the coming battles in France.

The new situation reports from Foreign Armies West coincided almost exactly with the information that the British were sending back to the Abwehr through the 'turned' agents. And slowly Richter's messages had concentrated more on the location of units than their strengths and arms. With 2,000 miles of coast to defend, the Germans were desperate for information on where the main landings would be. Hitler was still pulling out divisions from France to try and stop the Russians' advance. Rommel was sure that the landings would be at the mouth of the Somme to capture Le Havre, and von Runstedt merely carried out Hitler's orders.

In the end the careful bluffs and counter-bluffs fed back to the Abwehr had little effect. Neither did the information from Foreign Armies West. The Abwehr was losing its fight against Himmler's take-over, and Hitler no longer trusted even the Wehrmacht. Intelligence from the Abwehr and Foreign Armies West lay undisturbed in Himmler's offices.

On 18 May, the Miller family celebrated the birth of a daughter, Penelope Ann. At the celebration party ten days later, Erich Richter was probably the only man who was relaxed and at ease. He was also the only man in the room who didn't know that D-day was planned for 4 June, seven days away.

Richter spent most of his time with Miller. Despite the age difference, the younger man became a kind of surrogate father for the man who was virtually cut off from any non-official contact. There were times when the German was deeply depressed and for a week or so he would live with the Millers, sharing their family life.

From time to time a girl was provided for Richter to sleep with, but beyond this he had no real contact with women. Sometimes a mixed-doubles was arranged at the tennis courts at Wandsworth and once or twice they had taken him for a weekend at a hotel in the country and one of the girls from the RVPS would join them. But it only emphasized the German's isolation. He had English lessons every day but he made little progress. His only times of obvious and genuine happiness was when he was part of the Miller's family circle. He happily spent hours playing with the baby and his affection was almost too much. She was the only human being who, he felt, didn't sit in judgement on him. He was just another pair of arms and a voice – neither a traitor nor a security risk.

On 4 June the Fifth Army took Rome but it was two days later before the landings in France. On 20 July von Stauffenberg's attempt to assassinate Hitler failed. The Gestapo arrested over 7,000 people and it marked the end of the Abwehr.

The free world watched with bated breath as the Allied armies fought their way across France and the Low Countries. For the first time in over four years it looked as if the war could be nearing its end. The unbelievable was going to happen. Hitler and the Nazis were going to be defeated. Country after country was liberated and even the cautious British public began to feel that victory was in sight.

V1s and V2s were still raining on London but there was a mood of optimism. That optimism ended on 16 December when the Germans launched their counter-offensive in the Ardennes.

In Yalta, the three Allied leaders planned for Germany's unconditional surrender. And while their inhabitants asked for nothing except peace, in Whitehall, Washington and the Kremlin, men planned their countries' moves and counter-moves in the coming struggle for power. A sick American president who had only weeks to live gave the Soviets seven or eight nations as a gesture of goodwill, and more realistic men in Whitehall began planning for a wide variety of contingencies. Contingencies that ranged from political assault by the Soviets on the countries still free of their yoke to actual attack by the Red Army on its recent allies.

Germany itself was a heap of rubble, without government or law, and in their separate zones the former Allies created new societies in their own images. In the twilight of the Gods new gods were born.

After the German surrender Miller was instructed to negotiate some suitable pay-off for Richter and return him to civilian life in some acceptable role.

Miller invited Richter to their new home in Streatham. His wife and daughter were staying with his in-laws.

There was a thermos of coffee, two mugs, and two plates of sandwiches covered with damp cloths.

As he poured Richter's coffee and handed it to him, Miller said, 'I've been asked to thank you officially for your co-operation, Erich.'

The German shrugged. 'What happens next?'

'That's very much up to you. If you want to stay in this country we'll give you a new identity and British nationality. If you want to go back to Germany we'll give you complete documentation under a new name and every help with the authorities.'

'Can you get me a job here?'

'Of course. And there's a gratuity of two thousand pounds that can be paid in pounds or dollars, whichever you prefer.'

'I'll stay in this country then. It'll be safer.'

'What kind of job do you want?'

'I've no idea.'

'Have a think about it. Colonel Mayne says that he is coming down to see you in a couple of days' time. He'll be responsible for your new identity and the payment of the gratuity.'

'Who is he?'

'He's a very senior officer. A nice man. You'll like him.'

'What are *you* going to do?'

'I haven't really thought about it. There's still the Japanese war to finish so I expect I'll be in the army for some time yet.'

Richter sat back in his chair. He sighed. 'I still can't get used to the idea that it's all over.'

'It *is* , Erich. And it's best forgotten.'

'How's the baby?'

Miller smiled. He was already in love with his small daughter.

'She's fine. They're at Hastings with Penny's parents.'

'Shall I be able to see them again?'

'Of course. You'll always have a welcome in our home.'

Richter looked at him intently. 'D'you mean that or is it just English politeness?'

'Why shouldn't I mean it?'

'I'm a German, unimportant, a traitor. One of the losers.'

'You're not a traitor. The 20th of July people weren't traitors. They knew what Hitler had done to Germany.'

'By the 20th of July Germany had lost the war. When I came over, Hitler was still winning the war. That's the difference.'

'Draw a line under it all. It's finished. You've *earned* your British nationality, and that's more than most of us have.'

Two days later Colonel Mayne sent for Miller. He was waiting for him in the private office at the RVPS.

'Ah, Captain Miller, sit you down.'

As Miller sat down in the leather armchair, Mayne said, 'I've had a talk with Richter, he's changed his mind. Wants to go back to Germany. I'll fix it all up for him.'

'Why has he changed his mind?'

'Don't really know. Probably the call of the Fatherland. Roots, background, that sort of thing.'

'When's he off?'

'I'm taking him back with me tonight. Best to get him out of this place. Let him find his feet a bit and all that.' Mayne stood up. 'A couple of things. He wants to say goodbye to you and your good lady. He's become very attached to you both. When is she back?'

'On Sunday.'

'How about you come up to the War Office on Monday afternoon. Say at four. Ask for me. Room 417. Won't take more than a few minutes. Take one of the pool cars and a driver.'

Mayne headed for the door and Miller said, 'You said a couple of things, sir. What was the other one?'

'God dammit. Forget me head soon. Your name's in this week's Part 2 Orders. Promoted to Major. Well done.'

Before Miller could answer Mayne had gone.

As they came down the steps of the War Office, Miller turned to Penny. 'What did you make of that little episode?'

'He looked sad, or frightened, or something. Like he was being sent off to Siberia.'

'Jesus, it was eerie. Like a funeral without a coffin.'

'There were tears in Erich's eyes when he shook hands.

D'you think they've pressured him into going back, just to get rid of him?'

'Not really. They've nothing to gain by doing that. But old Mayne couldn't get us out of there quick enough. And that gloomy office. Ugh.'

'How about we eat out and cheer ourselves up?'

'Why not, sweetie, why not. We'll go potty and go to the Savoy of happy memories. When we get there, you phone your ma and tell her we'll be late, and I'll book us a table.'

The message from Mayne was addressed to Major Miller and was short and explicit. Every document and all material concerning Erich Richter was to be destroyed that day. There was nothing to be left on record of his war-time activities.

Sergeant Lowrey, Field Security, stood stuffing the papers into the shredding machine and watched carefully as the long curls of paper filled the metal container. He switched off the machine and emptied the shreds into the big paper bag, tied it with red tape, and pushed it to one side. The bags would be sealed by Major Miller, and Lowrey would take them to the incinerator in Block 4 and witness their final destruction.

The sergeant lit a cigarette and walked across to the long table where the rest of the material was laid out. Box files, buff-covered files, the red-striped Top Secret files and bulging brown envelopes. It looked like another four hours before he would need the major to apply the official red wax seals. He pulled up the bentwood chair, shifted the ash tray, and reached for one of the red-striped files to pass the time until he had finished his cigarette.

Part Two

Seven

He could see them through the wide glass panels and they had seen him too. Penny had lifted the little girl so that she could wave to him. As he waved back, the Customs officer said, 'Which flight were you on?'

'Air Canada from Toronto.'

Miller reached into his jacket again for his passport and showed it to the uniformed man. It was closed, but in the white oval which showed the passport number there was an 'S'. The officer glanced briefly at his face and then scrawled his chalk hieroglyph on the two bags without opening them.

The Airport Authority had let her park his car in the freight bay alongside the terminal building. It was 4 am and they hurried through the light rain to the white MG.

At the main roundabout he turned left. They were outside the cottage by the river twenty minutes later. He carried the sleeping child upstairs and laid her on the bed. He could hear Penny in the kitchen. He looked around the room. The rocking-horse, the shelf of dolls and cuddly animals that he brought back from his trips. This was the moment he liked most when he came back.

He would hear what they had been doing. The saga of cats and their kittens, the bonfire they had been invited to, the room that had been painted, the neighbour who had planted the potatoes and the man from the garage who had fixed the handbrake. But on his side there was nothing to tell. The food at some hotel, a mutual friend met in an airport transit lounge was the extent of his contribution. Even without the Official Secrets Act there was nothing he would have wanted to tell them. It was like being a man who lived his life in dark caves coming into a sunlit meadow. To be savoured but not inhaled.

His leaves were seldom longer than a couple of weeks. And although he would never admit it, even to himself, he was glad they were not longer. He knew that if he stayed longer he might never face going back. He wasn't afraid of going back. He wasn't afraid of anything, or anybody. But he was conscious of the pull of normality. Like a man remembering his childhood, it was always sunshine and summer when he remembered his time at home.

To an outsider his work could have seemed glamorous. The furtive meetings in back-alleys and nightclubs, the tracking down of a man, the silent midnight searches of empty offices or apartments, the use of extensive resources to ensure that some end was achieved. The unscrupulousness that came with the assurance that the end justified the means, no matter how ruthless the means might be. He and his colleagues lived in the world of real power and on his leaves he felt like a hunting animal living among its natural prey.

There had been a time, at the end of the war, when he could have got out. But it would have meant starting right at the bottom in some career. He hadn't known anything but the army and he had no pull towards any civilian job. In fact he was completely ignorant of what most civilian jobs entailed. To stay on gave him so many advantages: high financial rewards that were tax free; a position already well up the ladder of seniority; colleagues he knew and trusted. There were times when he wondered if part of the appeal was that it was all a bit like his life in the orphanage where you were looked after because you did what you were told. He was not unaware of the ruthlessness – his own, and that of the department he worked for. His masters were well aware of the doubts that assailed their field officers from time to time. It was part of their jobs to notice and to apply the mental Bandaids and bandages. The approach was always much the same. They were members of a club, an elite, who were privileged to know that the war had never really stopped. The target, the enemy, had a different name but the struggle was the same.

He gently eased the woollen dressing-gown from the small body, covered it carefully with the duvet and bent to kiss the blond hair.

She was standing at the bottom of the stairs, smiling up at him. Looking not much older than on the day they met. As his arms went round her she put up her mouth to be kissed. He held her close and it was minutes later before she pulled back her head and said, 'Let's go in the kitchen. You must be starved.'

It was a small, neat kitchen, bright and clean, everything in its place. As they sat opposite each other at the formica-topped table, she said, 'How long have you got, love?'

'A week. Including two days leave. Tomorrow and Monday. But I'll be back each night.'

'How did it go?'

'It's hard to say. Americans are friendly to everybody. I think they accept me, but they're very cagey about anybody from London since Burgess and Maclean.'

'She's been doing very well at school.'

'Does she like it?'

'She loves it. Hates holidays.'

'And how've you been, sweetie?'

'Not bad. Missing *you* though.'

He reached across the table and took her hand.

'Won't be long. Another three months and I'll be back

59

here for a year. And then only Europe on short assignments.'

She looked at him, checking his face.

'D'you like it, Dave?'

'It's all I know how to do, honey. But I don't like being away. I miss you both all the time.'

She stood up. 'You must be worn out. Let's go to bed.'

In bed, they made love and it seemed only minutes before the telephone rang. She got up quietly, put on her bath-robe, and went down to the hall. It was nine o'clock and the sun was shining. But she had shivered as she stood talking, looking at her face in the mirror.

She took him up a cup of coffee and saw the gun on the floor beside the bed, encased in its chamois leather holster, the narrow canvas harness looped round it.

As she stood there holding the cup some sixth sense pulled him back from his sleep. His eyes opened and his hand was half-way to the floor, reaching for the gun, before he recognized her.

She sat on the bed facing him, watching as he sipped the drink. As he turned to put the empty cup on the bedside table he said, 'What is it? What do you want to say?'

She wondered how he could come out of that deep sleep and 'know'. He spent his life 'knowing' before things happened. It was what he was trained to do. It was why he was still in one piece. Except for the long, jagged, white scar along his brown forearm and the cold hard look in his eyes when people talked to him. There had been a time when she threw small dinner parties when he came back. But she had given that up long ago. He listened intently to every word, but he never joined in. Their friends thought he was a pretty cold fish, strangers tried not to notice. It disturbed them too much. She had heard that one couple thought that he was a Mafia man. She had been amused at first, but later it had depressed her. It was too near the mark.

'What is it, Penny?'

'It's mother. Her heart's bad again. Dad says she wants me to go over right away.'

The cold eyes looked at her. 'OK. We'll all go over for a couple of hours. Has he called the quack?'

'She won't let him. She says it'll make her worse.'

'When were you over there last?'

'On Monday.'

'D'you tell her that I was on my way back?'

'Yes.'

'Did you tell her when?'

'Yes.'

She saw the anger in his eyes and round his mouth.

'Get Penny Ann ready then, and I'll get the car out.'

She sighed deeply. 'She wants me to go on my own.'

'And you agreed?'

She nodded. 'Yes. I thought you might like to spend a day with Penny Ann.'

'I've been away three months, Penny, and that evil bitch tries to cut us up the very first day I'm back.'

'She's ill, Dave, not evil.'

'She's sick, my love. Not her heart, but her mind. It's just a power play.'

'If you insist, I won't go.'

He looked at her white, drawn face, her anxious eyes, and he knew he couldn't refuse. She had to live her own life when he was away. No wonder she obeyed when that domineering woman snapped her fingers to prove that she still held the strings. He would change all that once he was back.

'What time will you be home?'

'She wanted me to stay overnight . . . ' She saw the sudden flash of open anger on his face. ' . . . but I'll be back by eight.'

'Is that a promise?'

'Of course.'

'And that will be it, for the week I'm here?'

'Yes.'

She phoned her father to come over, and before he came, Miller drove off to London in the MG, the little girl chatting beside him.

At weekends, the Science Museum and the National History Museum in Kensington cater for two entirely different sections of the public. Saturday is family day. Mothers and fathers point out great-crested grebes, and children press buttons that make engineering models work in their glass cases. Mothers knit on the brown, wooden benches while fathers explain the solar system.

On Sundays, the two museums cater for the walking wounded. Divorced or separated fathers generally end up with Sunday as their access day to their children. Conversations are difficult and stilted. 'She' has warned the child not to answer questions. Embarrassed, uneasy children can't remember how they got on at school or what other presents they had for Christmas. Too many ice-creams is reckoned to be bribery or 'spoiling', and fit men find a desperate need to sit down. On Sundays, a normal family driven in by the rain can feel much like a cat at Crufts. Those few hours that are so looked forward to become a desert of grey sand, a mental gymkhana, the wages of guilt.

Dave held his small daughter's warm hand as they looked at the whales. There was only an hour to go before they would drive back. They had eaten baked beans on toast for lunch in a café in Kensington High Street, and he realized how far away he was from the little girl. He knew about what the Russians were up to in Egypt, and what was really going on behind the scenes in Korea. But he knew almost nothing of the daily life of his wife and daughter. She thought he was joking when he seemed not to know about Babar and Asterix.

She was disappointed when they got back to the house and her mother wasn't there. But he made up for it by promising to read to her until eight o'clock when Penny would be back.

He read for at least ten minutes after she was asleep and then he laid her back against the soft cushions on the sofa.

At nine, he was tempted to phone, but pride and anger prevented him. By ten, his anger was cold and real, but under control. Lodged in his mind, part of his data-bank, never to be forgotten, stored up for use.

It was almost eleven when he heard the car door slam and her feet running up the garden path. He was stirring the sugar in his coffee as he heard her key in the lock.

When she saw his face as she went into the kitchen she knew there was nothing she could say.

'Where's little Penny?'

'Asleep on the sofa.'

She turned slowly and went back into the living room and he listened as she carried the child upstairs. They didn't make love that night.

Gisella Harting was twenty-seven, a spinster. And in post-war Germany that meant she was almost certainly going to stay a spinster. There were five women for every man. If you were unmarried and had no man by the time you were twenty-seven you would need to look like Ingrid Bergman to alter your status.

Although Fräulein Harting was no Bergman she had her attractions. Her big, luminous, grey eyes offset the heavy jaw, and her nose was snub even if it was a little on the large side. When she smiled, which was unfortunately seldom, the two deep dimples at her mouth made her look appealingly babyish. And in any other community her long shapely legs and her full, firm breasts would have attracted lovers if not husbands.

She had thought that her months at SHAPE HQ in Paris would have made a difference. But the aura of the German spinster seemed to have stayed with her. There was a translator there, a Hungarian refugee, who talked to her sometimes when she took the top-secret papers to the

Slav-language translation section. And then, almost over-night, she had been transferred to NATO HQ.

She had gone through yet another probing security check because her new job covered even more confidential work than her previous one. Her pay went up by two grades and she moved to a three-roomed apartment that she kept spotlessly clean and neat. She gave small dinner parties for other girls in the secretariat and was much respected for both her status and her efficiency. She seldom left her office before 7.30 pm, and when weekend work was necessary she made no complaint.

The times that she dreaded were weekends and public holidays, when her loneliness was emphasized by her colleagues' eagerness to be home to enjoy the parties and picnics. To go back to that empty flat, where everything was exactly as she had left it that morning, and to know, as she closed the door behind her, that she would be alone for two or three days, brought on a lethargy and depression that, from time to time, had made her contemplate taking her life. Her colleagues saw not the slightest sign of the quiet desperation behind her amiable, friendly façade.

Frith Street in Soho looks its genuine seedy self in the daytime. Only its ethnic restaurants give it life and authenticity. Many of them are highly rated by those who appreciate foreign gourmet cooking. But at night it changes its character. Not for the better. Just a different character. A different kind of seediness. The garish lights and the neon signs point to the clubs in basements and up rickety stairs. Their names and sites changing from month to month as the Vice Squad, the Drugs Squad, or the local police quite properly use the law to try to prevent their survival. Laws dating back to the early 1800s are invoked in the struggle, and sharp solicitors in Mayfair bend their minds to the precise definition of what constitutes a brothel or the performing of 'a lewd act'. Lewis Stoner was one of those solicitors.

His office was in an elegant Edwardian house near Curzon Street, and the brass plate beside the door said simply, 'Lewis Stoner and Co. Solicitors. Commissioners for Oaths'.

The furnishings of the office were heavily traditional: a big, oak partner's desk; one whole wall lined from top to bottom with law books; a circular table in dark polished mahogany with six matching chairs; and the faint, pleasant perfume of cedar-wood cigar boxes.

He was dressed formally, black jacket and pin-striped trousers, and he fiddled with a gold-plated letter-opener as he looked across at his client.

'Have you got any idea why they came against you rather than Mr Cappa or the landlord?'

'They've done Cappa five times in three months, and he thinks they're worried in case he goes for them on police harassment.'

'Who is the landlord?'

'A Mr Constantine. I think you know him.'

Stoner ignored the implied question.

'Did you say anything when they charged you?'

'I just denied it and demanded to see my solicitor.'

'They've granted bail on your own recognizances for a hundred quid. Have you got it?'

'Not bloody likely, and I ... '

Lewis Stoner held up a white hand to cut off the flow. 'Jack'll put it up for you. I'll speak to him.'

'Yeah. But it's harassment, Mr Stoner. The girls don't take money for sex. The money's for the drinks. We thought that was the way ... '

'Money doesn't have to pass, Mr Lowrey. A brothel is "any premises, or part of premises, habitually used or resorted to by persons of both sexes for the purpose of prostitution or lewd practices". Anyway you'd best leave it to me. That's what I'm here for.'

'What'll happen?'

'You'll be fined a hundred quid and the premises will be closed.'

'Does that mean we've had it?'

Stoner smiled. 'Jack tells me that he's got another place he wants you to run in Greek Street. You'll be able to go back to the present place in three months.'

Stoner stood up to mark the end of the interview. He didn't shake hands and left Lowrey to find his own way out. He reached for the telephone and reported the interview to Jack Cappa. The man who paid him. The man who kept him supplied with sixteen-year-old girls.

Arthur Lowrey had also phoned Jack Cappa and had been given the address of the Cherry Club in Greek Street. He would be there for five weeks until the previous manager came out of Wormwood Scrubs. Assuming that he would get remission for good behaviour.

Lowrey found his small room at the top of the ramshackle building in Greek Street. He had a small leather case that held all his worldly possessions. There was a camp-bed, an old steel safe on the floor, and net curtains at the fly-blown windows. A couple of pin-ups were tacked to the back of the door.

He walked downstairs into the empty room that only came alive in the evenings. There were fifteen rickety tables each covered by stained gingham tablecloths. Battered table-lamps with frayed, pink shades provided the dim light that was all that was necessary. A bar stretched along one wall with its rows of bottles and glasses. There were three or four small rooms on the second and third floors each containing some sort of bed, a chair and a washbasin.

The whole building was under a demolition order from the local authority, but the wheels of local government grind slowly, and the order had already existed for three years.

Such buildings could be rented cheaply from their landlords for short periods. Fire Regulations could be ignored, and sudden closure by the police meant no more than shifting to some similar premises in the neighbourhood and moving back in three or four months time under a different name. The customers were country bumpkins from the provinces up for a football match, and foreigners looking for a girl.

The club opened its doors most evenings about eight o'clock, depending on the weather and the whim of the manager. Two of the girls would linger in the doorway and the glow of a red light from inside the club gave a promise that was only reluctantly fulfilled.

The girls were young and coarsely pretty, and their job was the traditional one in such places. They sat at the rickety tables persuading men to order drinks at extortionate prices with the promise of favours to come. They knew all the questions, and all the answers, and their chat was expert and effective. They were there to fleece the suckers whom they totally despised. They despised them not for their lust, but for their stupidity. They took it as perfectly normal that a man should want to have sex with a girl, but they despised the men who were fools enough to try to beat the club world. By the early hours of the morning, if the punter was persistent enough, and the money offered was ridiculous, they would go to one of the small rooms for a hurried act of sex.

Lowrey never aspired to own a club himself. He was well paid. He could use the girls, and he was protected against the law and rival syndicates. In his moth-eaten evening-dress he saw himself as a suave man of the world, charming the girls, and keeping the suckers in their place, with what he imagined was the same self-assurance as the *maître d'* at the Savoy Grill. Like many weak men he was self-important and self-preserving. His attitude to everything was influenced only by how *he* would be affected. For a few months after the war he had been stationed near Brussels, a sergeant clerk with a Field Security Section. He had made a few hundred pounds on the black market and lost it just as quickly when he was demobbed and tried his luck on the black market in London.

As one deal after another fell apart, he became something of a laughing stock among the other spivs. But Jack Cappa was a shrewder man than the rest of them. He saw in Arthur Lowrey the kind of man he could use. Lowrey was no wheeler-dealer, but he was active, he could get things done, once he knew what to do. And he was well-educated by the standards of Soho. He won all his arguments even if he lost all his deals. Cappa took it for granted that he wasn't honest, but he guessed that he wasn't professionally crooked either. He was just the kind of man to front a club once he'd been shown the ropes.

Cappa, being the kind of man he was, had waited a couple of months until Lowrey was completely wiped out. The timing had been perfect. To the hour. Word had come to him quickly that Lowrey was finally 'skint', and getting slowly and messily drunk in the Swiss Pub. He had waited in Old Compton Street until the landlord eventually ordered Lowrey out.

It was a Sunday night in November, and Soho was virtually empty as the rain swept across the streets. Only the real locals were about, huddled for shelter in shop doorways. It was like some old engraving of London. A scene from a Dickens novel.

Jack Cappa gave him a bed at the Green Parrot Club and the next day went with him to Burtons and bought him a suit and a second-hand dinner-suit in the market. But for a month Lowrey had been little more than a messenger. In the second month he had been sent daily round every club at 5 am to collect the night's takings. There had been several tests of his honesty until Cappa was satisfied. At the end of four months he was given one of the sleazier clubs to run as its manager.

Cappa worried about Lowrey's apparent honesty. Every man had a weakness, and he wouldn't be happy until he could identify Lowrey's. It didn't seem to be money, it certainly wasn't drink, and there were no signs that it was drugs. It was about two weeks later that Cappa identified the weak link. All the girls at Lowrey's club had walked out except one. Everyone in the business knew what that meant. It meant that the manager was screwing the girl who didn't walk out, and the others had left because they resented the manager having a favourite. All managers slept with the girls, but it was accepted that you spread your favours around. Neither Cappa nor any other syndicate operator saw sleeping with girls as a weakness. It could certainly lead to problems, but so could smoking. The weakness was to let a girl affect your work. He sorted out Lowrey's problem, read him a lecture on controlling girls, and gave him more responsibilities.

Eight

Otto Becker put the files in two briefcases, looked round his office, and then headed for his car. He usually looked forward to Friday nights. It meant two clear days without work. A couple of political groups to address but they would generally be locals.

Becker was a keen amateur photographer and a leading light at his local camera club. His landscapes carried off cups and awards most seasons. Like all the serious club members he processed his own films and did his own enlarging. His darkroom and his pristine Rolleiflex cameras were the obvious pleasures of his life.

As a Deputy Minister he was entitled to an official car but he preferred to set an example and use his own. It was a pre-war BMW, with low mileage and in perfect condition. The Ministry workshop looked after it well.

It took almost twenty minutes to get out of the city. Hanover was intent on reconstructing the bomb-damaged buildings and streets, to get industry going again. And that meant diversions all over the place. But once he was on the main road south to Hildesheim he'd broken the back of the journey. Another ten minutes and he was pulling into the rough courtyard in front of the farmhouse. He had rented half the farmhouse for the last five years. His half was almost self-contained, and he had paid for a separate door to be built for his side of the building. As a reasonably important local figure he was treated with great respect by the farmer and his family. A Deputy Minister on the premises was the best kind of insurance you could have.

The farmer's wife brought in his evening meal. He wasn't a Catholic but he always had fish on Fridays, and a bottle of Riesling or Thurgau. After he had eaten he took the two briefcases to the darkroom.

He hung up his jacket and prepared the bench with the tanks and chemicals on the right-hand side – developer, fixer, and the sink full of water. From the inside pocket of his jacket he took the narrow slip of paper and placed it alongside the enlarger. Moving the enlarger to one side he moved over the camera stand. Placing the Leica IIIa in the clamp he measured with a tape the distance from the film plane to the bench, and slightly adjusted the focussing ring.

Opening the first briefcase he took out a file and consulted the slip of paper. Two hours later, he had photographed forty-five letters and documents from the files, and the two 36-exposure rolls of Agfapan were in the developing tanks. He gave them an extra two minutes of developing time before he emptied out the developer and poured in the fixer. He didn't believe in stop baths, freshly mixed fixer ought to be enough. Half an hour later, he unscrewed the tops of the tanks and held up the spirals to the light. The grey emulsion was half-cleared and he put the spirals back in the tanks. When both films were fully cleared and thoroughly dried he rolled them tightly and slid them into the metal film cassettes. It pained him to roll the film so tightly. It was bad practice. It could so easily cause scratches on the soft emulsion, but it had to be done that way. That was how they always wanted it. And this was the last time.

After dark on the Sunday evening, he packed the two cases, his photographic hold-all, and the two official briefcases, into the boot of his car. Then he went to a performance of *The Czardas Prinzess* at the Städtische Bühne in Hildesheim. He was still humming '*Tausend kleine Änglein singen*' as he drove back into the courtyard just before midnight.

It was the Thursday before the news had leaked out and a government spokesman in Bonn admitted in a brief official statement that it was true that a Deputy Minister had defected to the East Germans. He confirmed that Becker had attended his office as usual on the Monday morning and had left for his home at the normal time. He had not been seen since.

The newspapers spent a few days speculating on the whys and wherefores, and official sources denied any possibility of a security problem. The transport ministry was hardly the place for state secrets.

A month after his defection the East German government arranged a press conference at which Otto Becker was paraded before the world's press. He refused to answer questions but made a prepared statement that for a long time he had been disturbed by the militaristic attitude of the West. He saw NATO as a major threat to world peace. He would spend the years left to him working in the interests of world peace and democratic socialism.

Three months later he was appointed Deputy Minister for Industry in the East German government. The appointment was the subject of brief comment by most western media. When, two years later, he was promoted to Deputy Minister for Internal Affairs with special responsibility for the Security Services, it made a brief paragraph in *Le Monde* in Paris, and *The Times* in London. It went otherwise unremarked. Otto Becker lacked the new political virtue of 'charisma'.

There was a heat mist coming off the lake in St James's Park and Henry Parsons pushed his glasses back up his nose to make sure that he didn't miss the others when they looked for him.

The Royal park was a place that was often used by officers of MI6 for informal meetings. It was within short walking distance of their own headquarters; its calmness, its English-ness, its almost majestic setting could sometimes add a touch of sanity to some of the more outlandish subjects that had to be discussed, from time to time, by SIS.

Neither of them was going to like his news. Baker would be particularly put out. He was a bit too much the knight on a white charger about NATO security. NATO was never wrong for Baker, and Parsons held that that wasn't a good stance for any liaison officer. It led to adversary argument and inevitable confrontation. And right was seldom might in their sorts of battles. Your political masters could easily throw you to the wolves because someone a thousand miles away was in a mess, and by sacrificing a pawn they could save a bishop.

Thurston was a horse of a very different stripe. He and Parsons were of an age. And round about fifty, age, in SIS, could be very nearly synonymous with wisdom. At least you tended to listen before you talked. Thurston was Winchester and Magdalen, in SOE during the war, then some mystery intelligence job in Germany with 21 Army Group, and now some kind of roving intelligence trouble-shooter for the Foreign Office.

And then he saw them both, walking together over the elegant bridge across the lake. Baker saw him as they got to the path and walked towards him.

Thurston joined him on the park bench and Baker pulled over a deckchair and settled down facing them. It was Thurston who set the ball rolling, his bushy eyebrows raised in query. 'Good news, bad news, or just news?'

'Bad.'

'What sort of bad?'

'There's a German woman in NATO HQ, in a highly

sensitive section, passing confidential stuff to the East Germans. She's been doing it for over a year. Maybe eighteen months.'

'If she is, she'll be under surveillance already,' Baker said dogmatically.

'Afraid not, Tony. I've seen her last five security checks and she was cleared every time.'

'Maybe your people have got the wrong name.'

Parsons sighed. 'She works for Planning Group Four. She's the only woman on their staff.'

There was a long silence while Thurston and Baker absorbed the news. Planning Group Four spent its time imagining every possible move that Moscow or any of the Warsaw Pact countries could make in Europe against the NATO countries. They were also responsible for evaluating the possible NATO responses and making a recommendation. After discussion and argument, a final decision was made as to what the actual response would be. If Moscow had that kind of information it would be like somebody playing poker while looking over the other players' shoulders and deciding their bets for them. Even Baker looked subdued. 'There's no doubt then, Parsons?' he said.

'None at all.'

'How did your people find this out?'

Parsons half-smiled. 'You know I can't tell you that, Tony. But it's a completely reliable source.'

'Do we know what stuff's been passed on?'

'I can't tell you that either. This is just to warn you.'

'What do you want me to do?'

'We want you to do everything you can to keep the NATO security boys off her back.'

'Do they know about her?'

'No. Not a thing. But we don't want her disturbed or she'll do a flit.'

'Is there anybody else involved?'

'Not in Group Four.'

'Aren't I entitled to be put in the picture? It's in my bailiwick after all.'

'Yes. I think you are, but at the moment we should very much appreciate your silent co-operation with us on this. And the less you know, the more help you'll be.'

Thurston smiled to himself. Parsons had a reputation for being an expert at smoothing down ruffled feathers. He turned towards him.

'I assume the Foreign Minister is informed?'

'Yes. Not the details. He doesn't want to know beyond the basic facts. If she did skip, the Germans would carry the can of course.'

'Have Bonn been told?'

'Absolutely not. They may be told when it's all over.'

'When what's all over?' Baker looked alert and curious.

Parsons turned back to look at him. 'Ten out of ten, my boy. The answer's – no comment. Do either of you fancy a pint?'

Neither of them did, and Baker headed off towards Birdcage Walk and a taxi. Thurston fell into step with Parsons as he made for Queen Anne's Gate.

'Who's taking charge of this little lot?'

'I am.'

'Why us. Why aren't the Germans or NATO dealing with it?'

'They don't know anything about it yet.'

'Not even the NATO council?'

'Nobody. Just us.'

At the edge of the park Thurston stopped.

'Let me know if I can help.'

'Thanks.'

There were geraniums in window boxes on the balcony that jutted out over the water. The big windows were wide open and she could hear the carillon in the square. She didn't recognize the tune. It was the 'Bluebells of Scotland'.

He had said to be there at seven, at their usual table by the window that looked out over the bend in the canal. It was already ten minutes past seven and she was worried. He was never late.

She always came to Bruges by train from Brussels, and he came by car and parked it near the Museum. Every week, for almost three years, they had had this rendezvous. It was what had kept her alive and sane. The talk about music and painting, poetry and prose, and then the lovemaking. There were things he did to her that had shocked her at first, but as the weeks went by it was she who wanted those acrobatic sensualities. If only he could get the divorce she would be the happiest woman alive. She wanted nothing more than to be Mrs Istvan Szabo, and she would do anything asked of her to achieve that end. Then she saw him, making his way through the tables, and he was smiling.

As he got to the table he bent down to kiss her and then pulled up a chair alongside her, his hand on her thigh under the table.

'How long have you been waiting, my love?'

'Not long. It doesn't matter.'

'I've got news. But let's eat first.'

In fact he hadn't told her the news until they were in the room at the *pension*.

She was sitting on the bed and he was standing, undoing his tie, then the buttons of his shirt, and she could see the thick mat of black curls on his chest.

He hooked his foot round the spindly leg of the elegant gilt chair, pulled it up to face her, and sat down, looking at her face.

'D'you *really* want to marry me, Gisella?'

'You know I do. There's nothing I want more.'

'I think ... I'm not sure ... but I think ... that it may be possible.'

She was trembling as she spoke. 'What about your wife?'

'They tell me they are so pleased with what we have done together that they will grant us this wish.'

'But your wife?'

'They have spoken to her. They have promised her certain things, if *we* do certain things. And she will agree to a divorce if these things happen.'

'What does she want?'

'God knows. They didn't tell me. That is for them to arrange. I don't care what she wants.'

'What do we have to do?'

'They want us to give up this work and go out and live there.'

'You mean in Moscow?'

'No, in Berlin. East Berlin.'

'But how should we live. What should we do?'

'We should be married. They give us an apartment. They give us both jobs.'

'What kind of jobs?'

'In the Ministry of the Interior. Me as a translator and you a consultant.'

'When would this happen?'

'Very quickly. They would like us to go in a matter of days.'

'But what about my apartment, the furniture and things.'

He sighed, and shook his head, bewildered. Shrugging his shoulders, his arms spread wide, he said, 'I thought you would be so pleased, my love. We can be married at last. And you can talk only of furniture.'

She reached out, pulling him onto the bed beside her, her arms around him. He saw the tears in her eyes. 'Oh Istvan, I'm so sorry. It was so sudden. I couldn't take it all in. But I'm so happy.'

His mouth was on hers and she lay back on the bed as his hand slid under her skirt.

It was nearly midnight as they lay together, each smoking

a cigarette. And suddenly she remembered. 'I haven't given you the film, Istvan.'

'You're right. I clean forgot about it because of my news.'

She sat up and reached for her handbag. She sorted through the feminine oddments and handed over the camera. It was a small matt-black Minox. The exposed film was still inside, unprocessed. As she handed it to him she said, 'Have you got the exchange camera?'

'No. They said you were to take no more risks.'

'How are we going to do all this?'

'They're making all the arrangements. You'll be compensated for everything you have to leave behind. You'll keep one small bag packed and hidden away. Be ready to leave immediately. In ten minutes, say. I'll be in touch with you myself.'

'You seem to know all about it.'

'I had to protect our interests, Gisella. I had to demand to know the basics.'

'And what about you. Is this what you want?'

'Of course it is.'

'I've heard it's very dreary in East Germany.'

'What do I care as long as we're together.'

'You're sure of that?'

Smiling, he pushed her back on the bed and pulled her body urgently to his.

She walked alone, next morning, to the station. And waited for the 7 am Brussels train. She was thankful that it was crowded, and she sat in the corner seat looking out of the window, totally unaware of the flat landscape and the early summer sun.

Gisella Harting was suffering those doubts that many people feel when some long desired thing is suddenly attainable. Whether it was a Ferrari or a wild-mink coat, a Hasselblad or a Cézanne, you have it. And suddenly the lust and tension are gone. It's just a car, a coat, a camera, a painting. So what next? You are still you. When she had got the job outside Germany it was because she hoped that she might meet a man. *The* man. And she had met him. Istvan Szabo was that man. He earned less than she did. He was attractive but not handsome. But he wanted her. And all those years there had been that bitch in the background who wouldn't give him a divorce.

He had shown her photographs of his wife. She had to admit to herself that she was pretty, and in the one where she was sitting on the beach the bathing costume revealed a nice neat body. She was eight years younger than Gisella Harting.

Now, suddenly, all her dreams could come true. So why the doubts? As the train pulled into the station at Ghent she looked at the faces of the waiting passengers on the platform. Perhaps they were part of the answer. They belonged where they were. They had backgrounds, families, relations. Her apartment was probably better than their houses but it wasn't a home. It was just the place where she lived. And except for her father in Düsseldorf she had no relations. She certainly had no background. There would be no coming back. Sooner or later they would discover what she had been doing, and that would close the frontier against her. To come back would mean arrest and imprisonment as a spy. She smiled as she thought of herself being described as a spy. A few photographs each month of their ridiculous reports. They were more like children than adults, with their childish war-games. What would be the SACLANT response to total jamming by the Soviets of radar screens in the area of Gareloch? What is the recommended response to Soviet low-level interference with ACE HIGH? Even the code names they gave to these things revealed their childishness. Stupid men playing crazy games.

As she passed through the ticket barrier she thought of what her life would be like without Istvan Szabo, and she took a deep breath and walked out into the crisp air and bustle of the capital. Even thinking those thoughts had been a disloyalty to her lover. He too had no real home or background. They would be family for each other. At least life was calmer and slower in the Democratic Republic. Everybody said so. Even some of the politicians in Bonn said that it reminded them of Germany before the war. They would be fine together. That was all that mattered.

The Palace Hotel in the Place Rogier competes successfully with its brash new rivals; its clientele value its good service, its excellent food, and its discreet privacy. Sales conventions are not catered for.

In one of its suites Istvan Szabo and Boris Chukovsky were not seeing eye to eye.

'Why wait for another three weeks, Boris?'

Chukovsky shrugged. 'It's the normal routine, Istvan. You know that. When it comes to the point of defecting, these women get doubts. Let them cool for a week or two and then they can't wait to come over.'

'But for God's sake, when she comes over that's the end of it. She doesn't matter.'

Chukovsky tapped the long ash of his cigar into the crystal ash-tray before he looked up at Szabo.

'It does, my boy. We're going to put on a bit of a show.'

'You mean a press conference and all that circus.'

'Yes.'

'But why?'

'They've got two of our people. They're interrogating them now. When they've got what they want, they'll announce the arrest of two Soviet spies.'

'Who are they?'

'You don't know either of them. And that's not the point. We want to have something that counters their announcement.'

'But the western press never run these things for long. The

80

general public don't give a damn about Soviet spies, arrested or not.'

Chukovsky smiled. 'They'll bother about one of these. Anyway ... ' he said slightly impatiently, ' ... that's how it's going to be.'

'What if she won't co-operate?'

'She will. There's a prize for co-operating.'

'What's that?'

'You, my boy.'

'Oh no. You promised ... '

'Don't argue, Istvan. It's already been decided.'

'I've had that stupid cow for years. It's too much.'

'You've had others too, Istvan. The ones you wanted. Tania, Natalie, and the girl from the Bolshoi you fancied. So don't complain. And it won't be for long.'

'How long?'

'Second week in September you come over the border together. We'll give her a suite in the Berolina but we shall make problems for you. You'll be out of the picture for a couple of days. But all your problems would be solved if she gives a press conference. Makes an agreed statement. Nothing very serious. She'll see you for a few moments in your cell, and then you'll be released. You have a couple of days with her to talk about arrangements for getting married. Then the blow falls and you're arrested again. We give her the choice. She can go back to the West, which she knows she can't do. Or we'll find her a job in Moscow.'

'Where's my next posting, Boris?'

'I heard that it was to be either at one of our training schools in Moscow as a senior instructor, or maybe London.'

Szabo sat in silence. Senior instructor would mean promotion to major, and KGB majors lived well. But the pleasures of London appealed too. Either way would suit him.

*

81

She saw the lights in the cathedral as they skirted the Place Sainte-Gudule and suddenly her confidence evaporated. It was no longer a plan, a dream, a pleasant prospect, they were actually leaving. In Paris and in Brussels she had always felt an outsider, a stranger, but she realized at that moment that Brussels was the nearest thing she had to a hometown. She knew the streets, the buildings and the city's daily life. She had views on the rivalry between the Walloons and the Flemings, and *anguilles au vert* had become her favourite dish. And the man beside her, the man who was to be her husband, seemed preoccupied rather than elated.

As they crossed the ring-road to the Chaussée de Louvain she looked at him from the corner of her eye. His head was back and his eyes were closed but she knew that he wasn't asleep. He had been in a hurry when he rang the bell of her apartment and had been almost angry when she protested that she had just made herself a meal and was hungry. He had insisted that they left straight away. She had grabbed her small case from under the bed, thrown in her current toilet things on top of what was already there and that was it. The phone had rung as they opened the door to leave but he wouldn't let her answer it.

She closed her eyes until the car had slowed down and when she opened them she saw the big black and white sign that said *Aeroport de Bruxelles National*.

Szabo had left her in the bar as he went off to check their flight and ten minutes later they were boarding the Sabena flight to Amsterdam.

At Schiphol they had had to wait two hours and Szabo had sat with her in a corner, obviously agitated, his brown eyes alert and watchful. When the Polish airlines flight to Berlin-Schönefeld was called he had waited until all the other passengers had been processed before he took her arm and headed for the ground hostess. He was obviously known to her and there was no checking of tickets or boarding cards, they just walked down the plastic tunnel to the aircraft.

The plane was half-empty and they had been given two seats at the far end away from other passengers. They were clearly being treated as special. But she felt as if she were almost a prisoner rather than the honoured guest that Istvan had said she would be.

When they landed at Schönefeld things improved. A Russian who spoke excellent German was there to meet them and he had a bunch of red roses for her and a box of cigars for Szabo. He was amiable and charming as he escorted them to the official car that was waiting for them.

They had been driven to the Berolina and taken up to the luxury suite on the top floor. There were more flowers for her and on the table were tickets for concerts and the opera and half a dozen bottles of champagne. The Russian, who said his name was Chukovsky, had insisted that they all had a celebration drink and it was almost dawn before he left and they were able to relax.

She had slept soundly and by the time she had bathed and they had taken breakfast in their suite she had recovered her self-confidence. A waiter had brought up a huge basket of fresh fruit with the compliments of the management. And ten minutes later, an envelope addressed to her had been brought up by the hall porter. When she opened it there was a thick wad of Notenbank Marks.

They had strolled down Karl Marx Allee and had sat over a coffee for half an hour, and by then Gisella Harting began to have a holiday feeling.

Back at the hotel they had telephoned room-service for a meal. They were half-way through eating when the two men walked in. One was wearing the uniform of the Grenzpolizei. And it was he who spoke to Szabo. 'Herr Szabo?'

'Yes.'

'Your documents please.'

'What documents?'

'Passport.'

Szabo had walked into the bedroom and had handed his

passport to the officer, who looked through it page by page. Slowly and carefully. Finally he looked up at Szabo. 'You are a Hungarian citizen?'

'Yes.'

'Your passport is not valid.'

'Why not?'

'It is two months out of date. And where is your visa for the Democratic Republic?'

'I don't need a visa. I am employed by the government.'

'What government?'

'This government. The government of the GDR.'

'So where is your employment card?'

'It isn't necessary.'

'What is the purpose of your visit?'

'I am accompanying this lady on instructions of higher authority.'

The officer looked at Szabo. 'Put on your jacket.'

'What for?'

'You are under arrest.'

'For what?'

'You will be formally charged at the court. Get a move on.'

'Officer. I think there is some mistake. I came in with Herr Szabo.'

The man nodded at the girl. 'There is no problem in your case, Fräulein Harting. You registered as a guest of the State.'

'But Herr Szabo is in exactly the same position.'

'In that case the magistrate will order his release.'

Szabo turned to look at the girl. 'I'll sort it out, sweetheart. I'll be back inside an hour. Don't worry.'

He kissed her cheek and left with the two men. In the elevator he turned to the uniformed man, smiling. 'You do it very well, Heinz, and the uniform fits you nicely.'

'Chukovsky wants to see you in the manager's office before you go.'

'OK.'

The man in the frontier-police uniform was an actor from the Komischer Opera who quite enjoyed these little real-life dramas that he was called on to play in from time to time. And he was glad of the vouchers they gave him to spend at the duty-free Intershop.

Szabo had spent ten minutes with Chukovsky going over the rest of the scenario that had been planned for the girl. Chukovsky was putting on a party for him that evening and had fixed him a flat in the same block near the park.

Nine

Gisella Harting looked up at Chukovsky, red-eyed, her cheeks wet with tears.

'But what has he done. There must be a reason?'

'Don't worry, *fräulein* . It will be sorted out in due course. There are always formalities.'

'But you said he was in prison.'

'Yes.'

'But prison's not just a formality. He would have to be charged with some offence.'

'There *are* charges. He has no visa. All that has to be sorted out.'

'But he works for you.'

'Not for me, *fräulein* . I'm a Russian.'

'It's all the same. He works for the East Germans.'

'Then there'll be no problem.'

She put her face in her hands and sobbed uncontrollably. He stood there in silence, watching. They certainly were pathetic these western women. They were always the same. If she'd been younger and prettier he'd have offered to take her to bed. No wonder Szabo wanted to see the back of her.

He stood waiting patiently. It generally took about ten minutes for the snivelling to stop, and then the charade could continue.

When she eventually looked up he fished in his pocket and gave her a handkerchief. He sat down beside her on the old-fashioned couch.

'Do you know any of the East German officials?'

'No,' she sniffed. 'I don't know anybody at all.'

'Maybe you could use your influence.'

She frowned, not understanding. 'What influence?'

'The work you have done for them. They value that highly.'

'So why doesn't Istvan have the same influence?'

'He was paid, my dear. You were not.'

'What difference does that make?'

'All the difference in the world. They have to be suspicious of people who are paid. They do it for money. People like you do it because they want peace in the world. We want that too. That's why you have influence. You will have many privileges.'

Fräulein Harting looked around the luxurious room. Maybe he was right. She turned to look at him.

'What can I do to help Istvan?'

'Are you sure you want to help him?'

'Of course. We're going to be married when his divorce comes through.'

'That came through almost a month ago. There's no problem there. If they knew that it was your wish to marry Szabo I'm sure that would be in his favour.'

'Who can I speak to?'

'I'm not sure. But I'll try and find out for you.'

'How long will it take you?'

He stood up. 'Ring for them to bring you up a meal. I'll be back as soon as I can.'

'You'll tell them I love him.'

'Of course.'

It was just over an hour later when Chukovsky knocked on

her door. He was with a well-dressed, important looking man.

As they walked over to the armchairs round the low coffee table, he had introduced them.

'Fräulein Harting – Herr Otto Becker, Deputy Minister of Internal Affairs.'

Becker bowed low and took her hand. She looked younger than in the photographs in the file. He pointed to one of the chairs and when she was seated Becker sat down opposite her.

'We are very much in your debt, Fräulein Harting. A recommendation has gone through for you to receive formal recognition of your services.' He smiled, and then looked solemn. 'But I understand you are concerned about the eventual decision regarding Herr Szabo. Is that right?'

'I ... he ... we did it together, Herr Becker. We were equals. In fact it was he who told me what sort of ... '

Becker held up his hand.

'You have no need to give reasons, Fräulein Harting. We accept you as a fighter for peace. Your efforts must be rewarded how you wish. I understand that you are considering marriage with Herr Szabo?'

'More than considering. It was planned.'

Becker turned to look at the Russian.

'When is the press conference scheduled for?'

'Next week. Wednesday, I think.'

Becker turned back to look at Fräulein Harting.

'We have planned a proper welcome for you, *gnädige Fräulein*. A small celebration so that you can meet the press. Say a few words. Meet some new friends. Maybe we could bring that forward.' He turned to Chukovsky. 'How soon could it be, Boris?'

'In two days' time if you insisted, Herr Deputy Minister.'

'So. I insist. And immediately that is over you take our friend here to her man. He is released, and they are helped to make the arrangements for their marriage.' He turned to the woman. 'There are several departments interested in employing you, but that can come later.'

He stood up and bowed. 'Boris will continue to look after you, Fräulein Harting.'

After he had let Becker out, Chukovsky came back smiling. 'There you are. What did I say? You have influence, my dear. Deputy Ministers come running to please you.'

The huge auditorium at the East Berlin TV centre was crowded. At least four hundred men and women from the world's media were there. Chukovsky's hand pressed lightly against her back as he guided her over to the cluster of microphones around the podium. The TV lights prevented her from seeing the faces of the audience but she was aware of their clamour, and then the sudden silence as Deputy Minister Becker introduced her. 'Ladies and gentlemen, we have asked you here this afternoon to meet Fräulein Gisella Harting, who has recently decided to join us in our struggle for peace.

'For some years, Fräulein Harting was employed by a secret section of NATO. A section responsible for planning the eventual attack by the West against the Warsaw Pact countries including the Soviet Union. Day after day, these so-called experts plan the slaughter of innocent people. Making their calculations in millions dead and more millions maimed. All this just a few months after the United States signed, with the Soviet Union, a treaty to ban the testing of nuclear bombs. All this while the western press ask why the Soviet Union needs to deploy defensive forces to assist its friends of the Warsaw Pact countries to defend their borders.

'Even now, there will be representatives of the media, here in this hall, ready to dismiss all this as a figment of Moscow's imagination. And perhaps even the more independent among you may feel that there is some element of exaggeration. For all of you – the impartial and the cynical – we have prepared a press-kit which includes photographs of an actual document produced by the section which goes under the name of Planning Group Ten at NATO headquarters in Brussels. Ladies and gentlemen, that document is dated June of this year. It is signed, the name is clear, the officer concerned is identifiable. The handwriting can be compared. The reference number of the file and the report are clearly identifiable.

'At nine o'clock this evening, I shall talk with Fräulein Harting on TV. *She* is no figment of our imagination. Her previous status at NATO HQ can be checked. Her concern for peace, for the lives of everyone in Europe, and generations to come, deserves the highest praise ... ' He motioned Fräulein Harting to the microphones. 'Ladies and gentlemen ... Fräulein Gisella Harting.'

Her voice was so low as she read her short speech that the engineers had had to turn up the amplifiers. But few of the journalists were listening. Her piece was bound to be in the press-kit that they had been given, and they wanted to describe her, what she looked like, what she was wearing. When she lifted her head as she finished, flash-guns were firing hopefully from all sides.

Parsons' man, the Berlin stringer for one of the wire services, had read over to him both speeches verbatim, and had given him the reference number of the document in the press-kit. He also reported that even the journalists from extreme right-wing newspapers were shaken by the information provided. He had sounded faintly annoyed or disappointed by Parsons' lack of excitement. When asked what his own reactions were the journalist's comments were brief. 'I think you're all in the shit. Right up to your eyes.'

Government press-officers did their best to play down the story. Ministers racked their brains to think of something that could push the stories off the front pages. The Foreign Office and the Deputy Secretary-General of NATO issued bland denials and hinted at forgery. So did every NATO prime minister and the United States' Secretary of Defense. The lines to Brussels 241.00.40 were overloaded twenty-four hours a day for ten days.

In the UK, not only the serious nationals, but the populars too, kept the story on their front pages for ten days, and the East German government film unit had obligingly sent out film prints of the whole of the press conference. Both BBC TV and ITN had used clips in their news bulletins, and both networks had covered the item in depth on their current affairs' programmes.

Jack Cappa invited Lowrey for a drink and a talk at his flat in Shaftesbury Avenue. Cappa owned several flats in London and a big country house in Essex. He never invited anyone to his house. Lowrey had heard that he had a pretty wife and two small children, but he never mentioned either them or the house. Rumour also said that he was Master of the local hunt.

From time to time Cappa invited one or other of his henchmen for a chat and a drink. It usually had no more significance than a Royal Garden Party, and its objects were much the same. A small recognition of loyalty and good work, and a way of encouraging it to continue.

Cappa leaned back relaxed on the massive settee, a glass of Guinness in his right hand. There was lipstick on his left cheek and on his chin, and his left hand was comfortably cupping the breast of the girl sitting beside him sipping a port. The TV was babbling away in the background.

'You should have a good night at the club on Saturday,' Cappa said. 'United are at Highbury and Liverpool at Stamford Bridge.'

'Yeah. And there's a sales conference at the Regent Palace

on Thursday. But their hotel security people are watching the girls like hawks these days.'

Cappa shrugged. 'Send Ernie in with photos of the girls.'

'They've got their eye on Ernie too.'

'Sod 'em. They can't touch him if he just goes in the bar for a drink and 'appens to chat to a couple of the lads.'

Cappa's hand had slid up inside the girl's sweater and was squeezing the big mound slowly and sensuously. And discreetly Lowrey had looked over at the television. There was a close-up of a man's face. A face he knew. But he couldn't think who it was. The camera backed off and he saw a girl at an array of microphones. She was speaking in German and a voice-over was translating it into English. When he looked back at Cappa, he was grinning at him.

'You 'aven't met Julie 'ave you, Arthur?' He turned to the girl. 'He's one of my best men, Julie. You take notice of what he says. When he talks he talks for me.' He turned back to look at Lowrey. 'She wants to work for me. How about you take her back to the Ruby Club with you.'

Lowrey nodded. 'OK boss.' He took the hint and stood up to leave, and the girl went into the bedroom for her case and her coat. When they were alone Cappa grinned and nudged him in the ribs. 'Put her on the door, fella. Those tits'll bring in the waverers. Only eighteen, but she'll let you bang her all night if you want.'

Lowrey had had a busy evening. Not a good busy evening. Just busy. There had been four fights, and the bouncer himself had had to have seven stitches in his head. Over two dozen glasses had been smashed and a couple of the tables would have to be written off.

By four o'clock in the morning he was alone in the smoky club-room, sitting at one of the tables as he poured himself a cup of tea from the thermos. He couldn't close because three of the girls were upstairs in the bedrooms earning the jam for their bread and butter. Sighing, he got up and walked over to switch off the deafening sound of the Beatles.

On his way back to the table, he picked up a discarded copy of the *Evening Standard*. As always, he read the stop-press first. Stock market prices had gone up and some big-wig had been knocked off in Saigon. He turned to the front page. Spread right across it was the girl at the microphones and beside her was the man. And this time he recognized him right away. It was the kraut from the RVPS. He couldn't remember his name. But it wasn't Becker, which was the name they gave in the paper. He read the main copy carefully. He was a bloody politician now. A Deputy Minister in charge of Internal Security. He closed his eyes and tried to work out whether the German Democratic Republic was our one or their one. He racked his brain to try and remember the other name. Then he remembered. It was the German Federal Republic. Trust those other bastards to call themselves democratic. He turned back to the picture. The kraut looked as if he was doing all right. Good suit, and a ring on his finger with a stone that looked like a diamond.

He nodded to the punters as they left and the girls paid over to him half their money. He went through a couple of handbags just to keep them on their toes, and he told Julie to stay behind.

She was quite pretty. A bouncy young blonde, long-legged and slim except for those sensational tits. When he had locked up and slid over the massive bolts on the outer door he had put his arms round her and kissed her so that her head went back, the way Clark Gable always kissed them. But Julie was more of a realist, and she stood with her long legs apart because she knew from experience what happened next.

On the bed upstairs, Julie had let him enjoy what are known in show business as 'management privileges', and these, added to his previous exhaustion, left him wide awake and restless when she finally succumbed to sleep. He sat on the edge of the bed, his body tired but his mind grinding away. He reached over for the black, metal cash-box and counted the money. They'd taken £754, not counting the money from the girls. He closed the box, and as he reached over to put it back he saw his leather case. Slowly and quietly he opened it and sorted through the jumble of his worldly possessions. It was right at the bottom and he pulled out the brown file and closed the lid of his case.

There was his passport, his birth certificate, his National Health cards, an expired driving licence. His mother's death certificate. A red income-tax demand for 1951/52 and his army discharge papers. Two insurance certificates for a £300 and a £150 life cover. Ten pounds worth of War Savings Certificates, and a bundle of forged petrol coupons. Half a dozen letters from solicitors, two photographs of naked girls and then the buff envelope he was looking for. It wasn't sealed and he slid the two papers out. He opened them and read them carefully. Then he read them again.

He looked up slowly, staring at the wall as he sat there thinking. He was right. The man's name wasn't Otto Becker, it was Erich Richter. He was a commie now, a Deputy Minister, and that meant he was important. And he wouldn't want the world to know that he was a traitor who co-operated with the enemy to save his skin. He remembered, too, something that Cappa had once said, 'It isn't earning what matters, kiddo, it's capital, ready cash. That's what gives you power. And when you've got power you can tell 'em all to get stuffed.' And this could be his chance to get some capital. The documents weren't copies, they were originals – War Office paper, signatures, names, the lot. Admittedly, they were a bit yellow round the edges but you'd expect that after all those years.

Slowly he pushed them back in the envelope, and then he stood up and tucked the envelope into the inside pocket of his jacket where it hung behind the door.

He shoved the girl over towards the wall and slid in beside her, his hands reaching round for her breasts. She moaned softly in her sleep, but she didn't wake up. She was used to being in bed with men, and once she was asleep she didn't mind what they did so long as they didn't wake her up.

Ten

It took Lowrey eight days to get his passport fixed and for Cappa to arrange a replacement at the Ruby Club. He had told him that he wanted a holiday.

He had never been on a plane before but the flight from Heathrow to Tempelhof was uneventful. He got the name and address of a small *pension* from the information desk at the airport and stood in line for a taxi.

The *pension* was in one of the small streets off Prinzenstrasse, obviously rebuilt since the war but still with an old-fashioned look. It was a grim, grey day even for mid-November, but the lights from the *pension* looked friendly and welcoming.

He took a room on the first floor. It was a pleasant contrast to the grubby rooms he normally lived in. The furniture was modern, the linen was fresh and clean and there was a full-sized, framed, colour print of Van Gogh's sunflower on the wall facing the bed. There was a pay-phone on the wall beside the door, and a telephone directory. He took the slip of paper from his jacket pocket and checked the number again. There was no answer when he dialled. He realized that it was early for a club to be open and he took off his shoes and lay on the bed, his eyes closed.

Ten thousand pounds was the pay-off that he had first thought of, but it seemed a bit too ambitious. Five thousand was reasonable, but it might take time for the German to get it together in cash. East Germans were very strictly controlled and even a Deputy Minister might have difficulty in getting that amount through the check-points. That bloody wall was the problem. But that would be Richter's problem not his. Three thousand was more like it. He settled on three thousand. To be paid in US dollars.

When he rang the club again at 4 pm it was Charlie himself who answered the phone. Lowrey recognized the voice despite the German words. Charlie Laufer had been one of Joe Cappa's men before he put together enough money to, strike out on his own. He was originally German so he had headed for Hamburg and ended up in Berlin.

'Is that you, Charlie?'

'Who's that, Sergeant Flemming?'

'No. It's Arthur. Arthur Lowrey.'

'Who ... Jesus ... Arthur ... where you speaking from?'

'I'm in Berlin.'

'You working here?'

'No. Just visiting.'

'Come on over, mate.'

'Where is it? Where do I ask for?'

'Ask for Club Vogel. Off the Kurfürstendamm.'

'Half a tick. How d'you spell that?'

Charlie was dressed in a well-cut, dark grey suit. Almost unrecognizable in his obvious prosperity. His welcome was warm and seemingly genuine, and he took Lowrey into his smartly furnished office at the back of the bar. They sat drinking whisky and reminiscing, like veterans from some long forgotten war. It was almost an hour before the gossiping was done.

'What are you doing here, Arthur? Nobody comes to Berlin for a holiday.'

'I've got a bit of business. Some money to collect as a matter of fact.'

'You made it then?'

'I'm getting by.'

Laufer saw the comment as a businessman's caution, and maybe even modesty. He grinned across the table.

'How long you going to be here?'

'A few days.'

'Can you hang on here this evening?'

'If you'll have me.'

'Of course I'll have you. Let me show you around.'

'I got a problem, Charlie.'

'Tell me.'

'The guy who owes me the cash is over the other side. In East Berlin. I don't know how to get the dough out.'

'How's he paying you?'

'I haven't decided yet.'

'How come an East German owes you money?'

'It's an old debt, Charlie.'

Charlie Laufer was a shrewd operator. You don't survive in the Berlin club business if you're not. He sat looking at Lowrey.

'You're up to something, Arthur. What is it?'

'I'll tell you some other time.'

'It's up to you, friend. Let me show you round the club.'

It was a far cry from the Ruby Club. The red velvet, the smartly dressed bartender and the slowly changing lighting.

A pianist at a grand piano was playing slow jazz chords as girls moved round the tables with flower arrangements. The girls were young and pretty, and naked except for white bikini briefs.

'How much d'you make on the drinks, Charlie?'

'A hundred and fifty percent gross, and booze is sixty percent of our turnover.'

'And what do you make on the chicks?'

'Nothing.'

Laufer was grinning as Lowrey turned to look at him.

, 'It's not allowed. I've got a hotel next door. There's no screwing on club premises. The hotel is a separate company. It makes me five hundred US dollars clear. Every night. Six nights a week.'

'How many rooms?'

'Twelve.'

'How many girls?'

'Fifteen, sometimes twenty.'

'They're real beauties.'

Laufer smiled. 'Pick the one you want, she'll be on the house.'

Lowrey looked around the room, smiling, but his eyes were alert and interested, and Laufer learnt a lot from that look.

'The blonde sitting with the two guys with bald heads.'

'That's Magda. You'll have to wait until she finishes at two, so let's go back in my office and have a drink.'

'OK.'

It was nine o'clock the next morning when Lowrey got back to the Pension Allgau, and he desperately needed to sleep. When he awoke at four in the afternoon, there was heavy rain beating on the window, and he felt cold and stiff. And his mind was still fuddled from the drink and the lack of sleep.

Even after he had washed and shaved he felt no better, and he had no idea of how to contact Richter. He dialled Charlie's number and a girl's voice answered. He asked for Charlie, and when Charlie picked up the phone, he obviously knew who was calling him.

'How you feeling, Arthur?'

'I want to see you, Charlie. How're you fixed?'

'Come over here about six and I'll be free then.'

'OK.'

Charlie Laufer was too shrewd to ask any questions, but by the time they'd had a couple of large Scotches each, Lowrey was ready to talk.

'How much d'you want to help me get this dough, Charlie?'

'How much is it?'

'I haven't made me mind up. Say three thousand quid. Could be more.'

'You'd better level with me, pal.'

And Charlie Laufer listened intently as Lowrey told him the story. When he had finished Charlie looked across at him.

'You'll never get it on your own, that's for sure.'

'Why not?'

'Jesus. That man's the head of internal security. He's controlled by the Russians. By the KGB. He's a big shot. He wouldn't put a foot into West Berlin, and if you go into East Berlin and tackle him yourself you'll end up in the canal, mate.'

'So what do I do?'

'You got the letters. The originals?'

'Yes.'

And he slid the envelope out of his pocket and put it on the table. Charlie read both documents carefully and then put them back in the envelope. He looked up at Lowrey as he passed the envelope back. 'You'd better get two photo-copies done and then post the originals addressed to yourself somewhere safe.'

'Like where?'

'Poste Restante at the Central Post Office here.'

'Then what?'

'I'll want half of what you get, Arthur. But we'll be going for more than you wanted. Much more.'

'How much?'

'At least fifty thousand dollars.'

'Will he have that much?'

Laufer laughed. 'He'll find it, that's for sure. He isn't just going to lose his job you know. They'd crucify him. Our lot would be delighted.'

'How do we do it?'

Laufer looked at him. 'D'you want Magda again tonight or would you rather pick another one?'

'I'd like the cigarette girl.'

Laufer smiled. 'You've soon found your way around, my boy. That's Heidi.'

'What time is she off?'

'You can take her off now.' He reached for a gilt key and tossed it on the table. 'Tell them you want Room Ten. She'll be along in about ten minutes.'

'What about this other thing?'

'I'll need to think about it. Come in and have coffee with me tomorrow morning about ten. How are you off for money?'

'I'll get by.'

Laufer smiled, reached into his wallet, and gave him a wad of notes without either looking at them or counting them.

'You can settle up when we've got the dollars.'

'You think we will?'

'Too bloody true we will.'

Otto Becker walked back down the corridor to his own office, the thick file under his arm. Various people gave small bows to him as he walked, and he nodded in return to each of them.

The meeting was still going on but he'd laid down the guide lines. Two weeks before Premier Khrushchev's visit, every known trouble-maker was going to be behind bars. Not only in East Berlin but in every large city. There had been the expected protests from the prison authorities about lack of accommodation and he'd told them brusquely to put up wooden buildings and turn them into guarded camps.

As he went into his office he saw the red light winking on one of his phones. He took off his glasses before he lifted the receiver.

'Yes.'

'A personal call for you, Herr Minister.'

'Who is it?'

'I don't know, sir. I didn't ask. It's a man.'

'Put him through.'

He sighed as he waited for the clicks to finish and then he said, 'Becker. Who is it?'

'It's an old friend, Herr Minister.'

'Oh for God's sake. I'm busy. Who is it?'

'I used to see you every day at one time, Herr Minister, but that was a long time ago.'

'I'll transfer you to my personal assistant, he will help you if it's possible. What's your name?'

'Richter, Herr Minister, Erich Richter.'

Becker felt the cold spreading from his chest all over his body and for a moment he closed his eyes. He took a deep breath and decided to hang up. But he knew he wouldn't. He heard the quaver in his own voice as he spoke.

'What is it you want?'

'Money, Herr Minister.'

'For what?'

'Two old documents. One dated May 1945, and one dated January 1943. They're both signed by a Colonel Mayne. They're worth a lot of money.'

'Who are you?'

He heard the chuckle at the other end of the line.

'Don't let's play games, Erich. It's too late for that.'

'Where can I contact you?'

'Herr Minister ... ' the mocking voice went on, ' ... you know better than that. I'll contact you.'

'When?'

'Say about eight o'clock this evening.'

'I shan't be here.'

'Of course not, you'll be at home. In Leipzigerstrasse. We've got the number.'

The phone clicked and there was just the static on the line. He pressed the button for the operator.

'Where did that call come from, fräulein?'

'Just a moment, Herr Minister.' There was a few seconds pause. 'It came from West Berlin. A coin-box.'

'Did the caller give a name?'

'No, Herr Minister, he just said a personal call to you and we are not allowed to . . . '

He hung up. His hand wet with perspiration. It was a German all right. No mistaking that. But there was a trace of an accent. He lay back in his big leather chair. He said he saw him every day. Years ago. How many years ago, and where? He looked at his watch. It was almost six already. He felt faint as he stood up, and his heart seemed to be beating just behind his left ear. He took a deep breath and then phoned for his car.

Up to about five to eight he'd not been too bad, but at that point he started trembling and the cold started to spread again over his body. It was five minutes past eight when the phone rang. He closed his eyes and waited for seven rings before he picked it up.

'Becker.'

'We've had a little meeting here, Erich. We think sixty thousand dollars would be fair to both sides.'

'You must be mad.'

'Who would you like the photocopies to go to, Erich. Comrade Chukovsky or the Prime Minister? Or we could send them to both.'

'Photocopies of what?'

'You mean you'd like me to read them to you?'

'Yes.'

'It's on War Office paper. With a crest. Whitehall. The date is May 12th 1945. It's addressed to Major Miller, Intelligence Corps, Royal Victoria Patriotic School, Wandsworth, London SW. In handwriting it says "Dear Miller". Then it goes on . . . '

Becker couldn't bear it. He put down the receiver. Not

deliberately. It was a reflex action. Two minutes later the phone rang again.

'We got cut off, Herr Minister.' And he heard the soft laugh. 'Maybe one of your people. Tapping your phone.'

'What is it you want?'

'I've told you. Sixty thousand dollars US.'

'I don't have that kind of money.'

'Of course not. But you can get it. All those lovely roubles from Moscow. Don't tell me some of those don't trickle across into West Berlin.'

'I'll need time. Several days.'

Laufer heard the hardening in Becker's voice.

'You won't try to play games, Herr Minister, will you? That would be bad for all of us. No sixty thousand for us and a People's coffin for you.'

'How can I contact you?'

'I'll ring again tomorrow night. Same place, same time. *Aufwiederhören* .'

And the line went dead.

Becker went into the hall and put on his hat and his coat. He walked in the thin drizzle to the bookshop in Unter den Linden and pressed the bell four times. Three short and one long. A few minutes later he saw the lights go on and the old man came to the door and let him in.

Upstairs in a room that smelled faintly of incense they talked for a few minutes and then Becker sat at the roll-top desk and wrote. Again and again he crossed out words, but by the time he was finished there were still 143 words if you counted punctuation and figures.

He felt a lot calmer as he walked back to his house, and he barely noticed that the rain had turned to sleet.

Eleven

Dave Miller piled his fishing gear into the boot of the red Mustang. It wasn't really fishing weather and from the look of the sky it was either going to rain or snow. He stood back for a moment to look at the car again. He had bought it a month ago and it was his pride and joy. Whatever it cost he was going to take it back to London when his tour of duty was up.

As he sat behind the wheel, the engine running, he looked at the map again. He would have to get onto the Columbia Pike, turn off at Glebe Road and hit the Memorial Highway at the county boundary. Then on to Langley.

He had just gone through Barcroft when he reached to change the station on the radio, and as he turned the dial he heard an announcer's voice saying ' . . . shot in the head and his wife Jackie . . . ' And as he turned the knob hurriedly to get the station back again his bleeper came on.

He pressed 'Receive' and the red scrambler button.

'Miller.'

'Your people want you to go back immediately. We've booked you on to a Pan Am flight out of New York, and we've got a Cessna going to La Guardia in two hours.'

'Is it true?'

'Is what true?'

'I heard something on the radio about the President.'

'He's dead. Somebody shot him in Dallas.'

'Is that why I've been recalled?'

'I've no idea, buddy. I'm just duty officer.'

And the channel went dead. It was 2.45 pm Washington time, on 22 November 1963.

He had phoned Penny from Heathrow but there was no reply. Maybe she was already out shopping. When he phoned the duty officer he had been told to report in immediately.

The taxi dropped him near Queen Anne's Gate at 10.30 am and a car took him to the safe-house in Ebury Street. Parsons went with him. There would be a briefing meeting at 2 pm. He had slept until 1.30 and then phoned his home. There was still no answer.

Miller phoned home again, just before the meeting with Parsons. There was still no answer. Maybe she was at her mother's.

There was a room at the safe-house that was sometimes used for formal meetings. It had a long mahogany table and ten chairs spaced round it. Miller and Parsons sat facing each other. The table was bare except for a china ash-tray between them with the Dunlop logo in its centre.

'We've got a problem, David. We need your help.'

Miller nodded but didn't speak.

Parsons went on. 'Do you remember a line-crosser named Richter whom you controlled at Wandsworth?'

'Yes. I remember him well.'

'Have you any idea what happened to him?'

'He was going to stay in England, but he changed his mind at the last minute and decided to go back to Germany. I think he was pressured in some way by the DDMI at that time. I think it was Mayne.'

'He was given a new name, a new identity, proper documents and a first-class cover. I think you were responsible for destroying all his old stuff and our files covering him.'

'Yes, I think I was.'

'Did you do it personally?'

'I always sealed the bags personally after shredding, and I generally witnessed the incineration.'

'Who did the shredding?'

'God knows. There was a Field Security section at the RVPS. One of them always did the shredding.'

Parsons reached for the briefcase beside his chair, opened it and took out a newspaper. He opened it, front page uppermost, and slid it across the table in front of Miller. It was a copy of the *Daily Mirror*.

'D'you recognize anyone in that photograph?'

For a moment he looked at the girl in front of the microphones and then he saw the man. And despite the heavy glasses he recognized him immediately.

'Yes. That's Erich Richter.'

'If we hadn't been talking about him would you have recognized him?'

'I doubt it. I shouldn't have looked that carefully. It's just the usual huddle of people round somebody making a speech.'

'Read the copy.'

There were about a thousand words in the news story and Miller read them carefully, reading some paragraphs twice. When he looked up at Parsons his surprise was genuine.

'I can hardly believe it.'

'What can't you believe?'

'First of all, I could never have imagined Richter becoming a politician of any kind. Then, I can't imagine him defecting to the East Germans. And I certainly can't begin to see him as a Deputy Minister, especially in charge of their security set-up.'

'It's true. All of it.'

'He must have been more ambitious than I understood at the time.'

'Well, it's Richter who's got the problem. A real problem.'

'Serve the bastard right. Why should we worry?'

'Because he's our man.'

'He's *what*?'

'He's been working for us continuously. When he was a West German politician and since. He defected on our instructions.'

And suddenly Miller remembered that brief farewell interview at the War Office. The tense, sad-looking man. It explained a lot. Mayne must have put the screws on him. But it was very far-sighted on the part of Mayne and SIS.

'What's the problem? Have they rumbled him?'

'No. But somebody's threatening to expose him. A man who claims to have original documents on War Office paper, with Mayne's signature, that show conclusively that Richter was working for British intelligence during the war.'

'Does the man know that Richter's still working for us?'

'We don't think so. There's been no indication that he does, and several indications that he doesn't.'

'Like what?'

'He's asking for sixty thousand dollars. If he knew that Richter was still working for us it would be far more than that. And if he knew we were involved it would have been much easier for him to put the screws on us.'

'Maybe he's taking two bites at the cherry. When he's got the sixty grand he'll come back for the rest.'

'Maybe. But he speaks German. A slight accent, but Richter's sure that German is his mother-tongue. He speaks up-to-date, slangy, Berlin German.'

'What's the significance of that?'

'First of all, no German has been even vaguely connected with our running of Richter. A Pole who speaks very bad German is the only possible contact and he sent us the message from Richter. He's one of our people in East Berlin. He's Richter's normal contact point. The only time the documents can have been taken was when they were assembled for shredding. And all the people concerned were British, in the services, and with security clearance.'

'Seems that the clearance wasn't good enough.'

'Looks like it.'

'Let's go back over the RVPS records and check the lot.'

'There's not much still left, and there's only you who could make sense out of it.'

'That won't take long.'

'That's only the beginning. Richter wants out. He's shit-scared now, which is understandable. He's scared about staying, and scared about making any move to get out.'

'So?'

'The only person he trusts now is you. He wants you to get him out.'

'So give me a team. I'll get him out all right.'

'It's not that easy.'

'Oh come on. I've done it dozens of times in all sorts of places.'

'I know. The problem is that we want him to stay. For at least another two weeks.'

'But something could leak in that time. They could rumble him and he'll go straight in the mincer. He'll sing like a bird. What the hell can a scared man do in two weeks?'

'A lot, I'm afraid.'

'Tell me.'

'The girl in the picture. Gisella Harting. We knew she was passing information to the East Germans through a Hungarian KGB man in Brussels. It was Richter who tipped us off.

'When we first learned about this, she was secretary to Planning Group Four. They're a top secret section responsible for evaluating what the NATO response would be to any move by the Soviets or the Warsaw Pact countries. Right up to where the nuclear button gets pressed.

'This meant that the Soviets were able to read our cards way ahead of events. We were going to pull her in, and then an evaluation team came up with a better alternative. We created an even more top-secret outfit called Planning Group Ten. They did the same kind of work but included political considerations too.

'We transferred her to that. A promotion. But Planning Group Ten was a special deception unit. So she was sending back stuff that we wanted the Russians to see. We could afford to look much tougher, quicker on the trigger, than we could ever be in fact.

'There were some signs that she was going to defect, and we were getting ready to pull her in. She beat us to it and skipped with her boyfriend, the Hungarian. The Soviets put on the press-conference to announce her defection and almost at the same time Richter contacted us about the blackmail attempt. Khrushchev is visiting East Berlin in the next two weeks and we've heard that they're going to use his visit to mount a big campaign using a whole host of material the girl passed to them. We shall then reveal that it was a counter-operation against their espionage network. Some people will believe us, some won't. We want Richter to be there when they're reacting to our mission to check their next move. They'll almost certainly swear that we are lying and we hope that Khrushchev will stay involved. Then we bring Richter out and he confirms our story. Khrushchev is made to look a fool or a liar and the East Germans will carry the can. And a lot of heads will roll in Moscow. KGB heads.'

Miller slowly shook his head. 'Sometimes I wonder. Who's crazier? Them or us?'

Parsons smiled. 'That's just a sign that you're getting old, Dave.'

'You're damned right.' He looked at his watch. It was seven o'clock. 'D'you want to go on?'

'If it's OK with you, yes.'

'I'll go and phone Penny. I won't be long.'

He dialled three times to make sure there wasn't a dialling error but there was still no answer. He rang her parents' number and her father answered. '4951.'

'David here, dad. Is Penny with you by any chance?'

There was a pause.

'Hold on. I'll go and see.'

Miller frowned. Surely the old buffer knew whether his daughter was there or not. Then he heard her voice. It sounded strained and thin. 'Hello, David.'

'Hi. I'm back for a day or two.'

'So I heard.'

'What's that mean?'

'Felicity Parke's got a job at Heathrow. She said she saw you there yesterday morning.'

'I phoned home straight away. About nine. I couldn't get an answer.'

'I wasn't there.'

'Doesn't matter. When'll you be back home?'

There was a long pause before she spoke. 'I won't be back, David.'

'What's that mean?'

'You got my letter?'

'I got your letter with Penny Ann's photograph in.'

'I sent you another after that. Explaining.'

'Explaining what?'

'I've left you, David. I'm not coming back.'

'You're kidding.'

'I'm not.'

'What's it all about?'

'I'm tired of this life. Your job comes first, not us. You're never here. You're a visitor not a husband.'

'That's because of my job for God's sake. I don't like it any more than you do.'

111

'You could change your job.'

'And do what? I've got no qualifications for another job.'

'There are security jobs in companies. Industry and commerce.'

'You mean checking that the doors are all locked at the local factory? Me and a scruffy Alsatian?'

'Other men make sacrifices for their families.'

'By God, they don't make more sacrifices than I do. Living out of cases, going ...'

'You're upsetting her, David.' It was her father's voice. He had been listening on the extension.

'Penny, are you there Penny?'

But the line was dead. It was that old bitch. He could hear her words in Penny's words. Industry and commerce. Sacrifices. Just a visitor. He felt cold and suddenly lonely. He was used to being alone but there had always been that warm light at the end of the tunnel. His family and his home.

He walked back into the conference room.

'Everything OK?' Parsons said, without looking up.

'Yep.'

'You should be getting leave and your London posting when this is over.'

Parsons looked up when Miller didn't reply. Miller's face looked tense. But that was par for the course. It was why field-officers were paid well, in tax-free money.

'Where are you going to start, David?'

'On the Field Security section that was stationed at Wandsworth. They were Intelligence Corps and their records will be at the depot. I think it's at Maresfield in Sussex. I'll contact them.'

'Keep in touch with me. As often as you can.'

'OK.'

Twelve

Miller had got the nominal roll of the Field Security section. It gave their names, their service numbers and their ranks. The War Office records could only supply their addresses at the date of discharge, and that was years ago.

He put the names and addresses to Special Branch through Parsons. They had started with the officer commanding the Field Security section, now a solicitor. He had saved them hours of footslogging. He established that only two of his men had ever been responsible for shredding. He looked down the list and confirmed the two names. One was Company Sergeant-Major Hugh McIver, the other was Sergeant Arthur Lowrey. CSM McIver had died in a fire in Glasgow in 1952. Special Branch concentrated on Lowrey.

By mid-morning the next day, Parsons had phoned Miller. Special Branch had traced Lowrey to the Ruby Club and Parsons gave him Cappa's name, telephone number, and address.

Twenty minutes later he pressed the bell on the door of Cappa's flat in Shaftesbury Avenue. Cappa opened the door wearing a bathrobe, his hair tousled, his eyes half-closed.

'What is it?'

'Are you Mr Cappa? Jack Cappa?'

'Who are you?'

'My name's Miller. I'm a police officer.'

'You got a warrant card?'

Miller unfolded the half of his identity card that showed his photograph. Cappa looked at the picture and then back at Miller's face.

He shrugged his shoulders. 'What is it?'

'Shall I come in, Mr Cappa, or would you prefer to come to Savile Row?'

Cappa sucked a tooth reflectively and then slowly stood aside to let Miller in.

'Do you employ an Arthur Lowrey, Mr Cappa?'

'What's it all about?'

'I asked you a question, Mr Cappa.'

'And I asked you one.'

'Fine. Get dressed and we'll go to the station.'

'Are you charging me?'

'I'm taking you in for questioning.'

Cappa's hooded eyes looked Miller over.

'What's Lowrey done?'

'How long has he worked for you?'

'Seven, eight years, thereabouts.'

'Where is he now?'

'I've no idea.'

Miller saw the smirk on the man's face and said softly, 'You're sure you don't know where he is, Mr Cappa?'

'Quite sure.'

'I'll give you my card in case your memory improves.'

Cappa looked at the card, smiling as he lifted his head to look at Miller. 'It won't guv'nor. It won't.'

Two hours later, four of Cappa's seven clubs had been closed. There was a sheaf of summonses ranging from inadequate fire precautions to use of premises as a brothel for all of them. When the fifth club was closed Cappa took the hint and phoned Miller. Miller interviewed him at Scotland Yard.

'Where *is* Lowrey, Cappa?'

'He went off on holiday.'

'Where?'

'I don't know.'

Miller stood up briskly. 'Thank you, Mr Cappa.'

'Just a minute, guv'nor. He took his passport.'

'Where is he? Don't waste my time.' There was an edge to Miller's voice that disturbed Cappa. Whatever he was he wasn't an ordinary copper.

'I think he's gone to Berlin.'

'What makes you think that?'

'I saw his airline ticket.'

'What airline was it?'

'BEA.'

'What day?'

'A week ago last Monday.'

'What's his address in Berlin?'

'I don't know. That's straight, mister. I've no idea.'

'Does he know anyone in Berlin. Has he got any friends there?'

'Not that I know of.'

'Have you?'

'No.'

'Has he got any friends anywhere in Germany?'

'I don't think so.'

'And you?'

'No. None.'

'OK. You can go, Mr Cappa.'

Cappa stood up, his eyes on Miller's face. 'How about my clubs, Mr Miller. Are you gonna take the heat off 'em now?'

Miller smiled. 'I don't know what you're talking about, Cappa.'

An hour later Special Branch had passed Parsons the flight number, its arrival time at Tempelhof, and confirmation that the ticket covered return within thirty days.

Miller phoned Cappa, who seemed to have recovered his nerve.

'What does Lowrey look like, Cappa?'

'Average.'

'Colour of eyes?'

'Don't remember.'

'Height?'

'Don't remember.'

Miller paused. 'Just remind me, Mr Cappa, what's the name of your club that's still open?'

'Blue eyes. About five seven. Going a bit bald on top. Brown hair. Skinny.'

'Have you got a picture of him?'

'Why the bloody hell should I have a picture of him. We ain't sweethearts.'

Miller hung up. He'd asked for that. He phoned Parsons and told him he'd be out of contact for two or three hours.

He took one of the SIS pool cars and drove down the M4, trying to think what he would say when he got there.

There was a solitary sculler on the oily grey Thames as he drove over Marlow bridge. At the end of the High Street he turned left, carried on for a mile and then turned up the hill to the estate. As he slowed down to turn into the crescent he saw her father closing the garage doors. He was still fiddling with the lock as Miller walked up to him.

'Good afternoon, dad.'

The grey-haired man turned, startled.

'Oh, David. It's you. Penny's not here.'

'Where is she?'

'She's gone into town.'

'Where's Penny Ann?'

'She's with her grandma. I wouldn't disturb her if I was you. Children get upset.'

'Husbands get upset too.'

'I can't let you in, David.' And he stood in front of the door.

116

'Don't be silly, dad, Penny Ann's my daughter. I'm going to see her.'

'I can't allow it.'

'Open the door or I'll open it with my foot.'

The old man was trembling, saliva on his lips. 'You're a violent man, David Miller. My wife always said you were.'

'Are you going to open the door or do I do it?'

Muttering, the old man turned the key in the door. Miller walked in uninvited. Her mother was through in the sitting-room, knitting.

He could hear the thud of pop music from a bedroom and he turned and went up the stairs.

She was lying on the bed, her eyes closed, her long blond hair spread out on the pillow. She was nineteen, and gorgeous, and she was his daughter.

'Hello Penny Ann.'

She sat up suddenly, her hand to her heart. 'Daddy. What're you doing here?'

He smiled. 'I came to see you and momma.'

She frowned. 'She said you were being divorced.'

'Takes two to do that.'

'What about Peter?'

'Is he the new man?'

'Hasn't she told you about him?'

'No. Who is he?'

'He's a BOAC pilot.'

'What's he like?'

'A drip. But he's a pleasant drip.'

'Let's go and have a meal.'

'The old lady will have the vapours. But yes.'

She stood beside him at the door to the sitting-room as he spoke to her grandparents.

'Penny Ann is coming out for a meal, she'll be back in a couple of hours.'

The old woman's face was suffused with anger. She waved

a hand imperiously towards her husband. 'Ring the police, Edward. Tell them what's going on.'

Her head turned quickly at Miller's laugh, her eyes flashing anger. Her mouth twisted in a grimace, her hand to her chest.

'Oh, my God. My heart. My ... ' Her head slumped to her shoulder.

As if it had been rehearsed, Miller walked to the phone and dialled 999. As the operator answered, he said, 'Ambulance service please.'

The woman got to her feet and, her eyes blazing, she snatched the phone from his hand and cut off the connection. 'You utter swine,' she hissed.

Smiling, Miller turned and took his daughter's arm.

They ate at the French restaurant in Marlow, and there were many mistaken but envious glances cast towards him.

'D'you still like sorbet, daughter?'

'Afraid so. Lemon if they've got it.'

'Lemon it is.'

She looked at him fondly. 'How old are you?'

'Gee ... ' he closed his eyes, his lips counting silently. ' ... forty-two or forty-three. I can never remember.'

'You're a handsome man, pop.'

He smiled at her. 'Are you trying to say something?'

'I guess so.'

'Say it then.'

'She loved you a lot, you know.'

'I loved her too.'

'She didn't have much of a life without you.'

'I understood that. We discussed it before I signed on again after the war. There was no other job I could do that would give us a decent living. I had no qualifications. It was that or the police.'

'Did *you* get lonely?'

118

'I was lonely all the time but I thought it was worthwhile.
I guess I had to think that.'

'Have you slept with other women?'

'No. Never.'

'You must have been tempted to.'

'Physically I was. But not mentally. It would have been
a poor return for what your mother did for me.'

'What did she do?'

'Looked after you. Kept a home going. Waited for me.'

'She had all the pressure from grandmother. Week after
week.'

'She's an adult woman, she didn't have to go along with
it.'

'Did momma do the little girl act with her when you were
around?'

'Yes.'

'Didn't it make you despise her?'

'Who?'

'Momma.'

'No. I couldn't understand it. I just took it that she'd
eventually grow out of it.'

'She didn't. She never will. The old bag tries to turn her
against me, but it doesn't work. I'm not a man. And I know
how to handle it.'

'What do you think your mother wants?'

'I think she wants this Peter chap.'

'But he must be away a lot too.'

'Yes, but it's only a couple of days at a time. And he does
gardening and goes for a drink at the pub ... ' She smiled.
' ... I can't imagine you ever getting like that.'

'Why not?'

'You're too grown up for that sort of crap.'

'What would you recommend me to do to put it right?'

The blue eyes looked at his face. 'Truth?'

'Of course.'

'If it won't make you too unhappy, let her go.'

'Will she be happy?'

'Oh no. She'll just be unhappy in a different sort of way. With you she feels she comes a bad second to your work. And it's true. It makes her feel neglected, left out. She ought to have known that it would be like that from the start. But she didn't. Most women would feel the same. It's like women who marry alcoholics to cure them. It doesn't work. She's not very bright. She's just human.'

'How does the new boy get on with your grandmother?'

'He's doing fine right now because he's getting you out of the way. His turn will come.'

'And how about you?'

'I'm fine. RADA have accepted me. I start after Christmas.'

'Are you in love with anyone?'

'Kind of. But the acting is going to come first.'

'Will you come and see me as often as you can?'

'Are you going to be around now?'

'I'll be away for a couple of weeks or so, then I'll be London based.'

'It sounds horrible but it's meant nicely. I'm glad in a way that I don't know you all that well, because I like you apart from the fact that you're my father.'

'Why?'

'You're fishing. I don't know. I just like you. You're cool and calm. You know what it's all about.'

'We'd better go, honey.'

'I wish I'd got a recording of you calling for the ambulance. That was brilliant.'

He smiled. 'Come on.'

Thirteen

Miller landed at Tempelhof just after eleven, and there was already a sprinkling of snow on the ground as he crunched across to the waiting car.

The SIS house was in a tree-lined road running parallel with the Kurfürstendamm. Its high, wrought-iron gates and railings were backed by a thick hawthorn hedge, and the gravel drive swept round a well-kept, circular flower bed in front of the house itself. Previously owned by a wealthy wine merchant, the rooms were a little too large for its present purpose. And with a mainly transient population, it lacked personality.

The master room on the first floor was stacked with radio and other equipment. Tape-recorders, microphones, transmitters and specialist receivers filled the shelves, and there was a smell of ozone in the air. There was already a pile of messages for Miller and he sat in the radio room checking them through.

Richter had been told that Miller was on his way to Berlin and had agreed to stall the blackmailer as long as he could. The Passport Office had supplied a print of the photograph attached to Lowrey's passport application. There had been a call from Cappa who remembered the name of one of his previous employees who had gone to Hamburg. The name was Laufer. Karl Laufer. CIA Langley asked for his instructions on what to do with the Mustang. There were three personal letters for him which were being sent over on a routine RAF flight. Dollars, pounds sterling, and marks, were available from SIS Berlin for his operation and in case the blackmailer eventually had to be paid.

Lowrey's passport photograph had come through on the photoprinter, and he asked for ten copies to be blown up to postcard size. It was a nondescript face. The wary, animal eyes, the thin lips of a wide mouth, the hollow cheeks, gave it a ferrety look. There were faces like that in every city. Knowing, merciless, weak faces.

He waited for two copies of the photograph, and put through a call to the SIS detachment in Hamburg for them to trace Karl Laufer. He sent a signal to Parsons to see if Cappa could give a description of Laufer. And finally he put through a courtesy call to the name he had been given as his CIA contact for the operation. The Americans were handling the breaking of the news about Gisella Harting once Richter was over the border.

It was after midnight when he walked to a restaurant near Kempinski's and had a bowl of soup and a Wiener schnitzel.

He was in bed, almost asleep, when he remembered about the information desk at Tempelhof. The operator told him that it was closed until 9 am.

At the hotel next to Club Vogel, Lowrey sat on the edge of the bed watching Heidi Winkler undress. Cigarette girls were more elaborately dressed than hostesses, and her costume consisted of a black bra that pushed up her young breasts without covering them, a kind of ballerina's 'tutu', black stockings and a pair of lacy black briefs. It was almost five minutes before she was naked and Arthur Lowrey wasn't a patient man. But by now she was used to the Englishman's funny ways, and as he pulled her onto the soft, wide bed she opened her long legs automatically.

The boss had told her to keep him happy, and for a couple of nights she had gone through her extensive repertoire. But the Englishman had very uncomplicated tastes. He didn't like the fancy stuff. But what he did like, he liked a lot. She was too used to men and sex for it to turn her on, so she found the Englishman no problem. All she had to do was keep her legs open and lie still. And at reasonable intervals make those routine sounds that are meant to indicate rapture and satisfaction.

It was much later, when they were talking and smoking cigarettes, that she first realized he was getting serious about her.

'Why do you want to know, Arthur?'

'You and I might go into business together.'

'Doing what?'

'A club or a café. Something like that.'

She stared at him speculatively, wondering if it was the wine and the sex, or if it was real. 'Have you got money, Arthur?'

'No, but I will have soon. All the money we should need.'

'You'll never squeeze any out of Charlie, if that's what you were thinking.'

He smiled. 'It'll be me giving Charlie money, my girl.'

'But you don't speak German.'

'No need, honey. We'd be in London.'

'I'd never get a work permit.'

'There are other ways,' he said, smiling, his hand caressing her thigh.

'What d'you mean, Arthur?'

'If we were married there'd be no problem. You'd be as British as me.'

And before she could reply, he had pushed her gently back on the bed. As she closed her eyes, her mind was racing. It would mean at the very least that she'd get out of Berlin. She could always earn a living wherever she was. That was never

123

a problem for pretty girls. She would be British. And she'd be in London. He didn't look tough enough to run a club, but maybe it was different in London. She lay there patiently until he had finished and was reaching again for the wine bottle.

As he handed her a glass, she said softly, 'Was that OK, Arthur?'

He grinned. 'You're fantastic, kid. The best.'

'When do you get this money?'

He laughed. 'Don't worry about that, kid. It's men's stuff.'

She pouted prettily. 'You're just kidding me, aren't you?'

His eyes went to her face and then down her lithe young body. He'd never get a girl like her in London. He looked back at her face. 'Are you interested, kid? Really interested?'

'Maybe. But I'd want to know what the deal would be.'

'You and me, sweetie. Equal partners.'

'Properly married?'

'Of course.'

'Have you been married before?'

'No. I've been waiting for the right girl.'

'Tell me about the money then.'

He hesitated for a moment and then saw the sulky, disbelieving look on her face. 'You won't talk about it?'

'Of course not, if you say so.'

'Not even to Charlie?'

'No. To hell with him.'

'I've got the bite on a politician. A big man.'

She frowned. 'What's the bite?'

'I know something he doesn't want anyone else to know. He'll pay to keep quiet.'

'*Erpressung?*'

'If you say so.'

'Who is he? Have I heard of him?'

124

'I should think so. He's over the other side.'

'You mean he's Russian?'

'No. He's East German.'

'They can't even afford a good screw when they creep over to West Berlin.'

'This one can. He's a Minister.'

She shrugged. 'I hope you're right.'

'You're interested then, Heidi?'

She nodded. 'Of course I am.'

It was nearly 4 am before he had finished with her, and as he lay asleep beside her she weighed it all up and decided that she would do it. But she'd check first that he was on the level and that marrying him really did make her British. She knew who would know the answers.

She woke at two. Lowrey had gone. She bathed and then dialled a number. She put on her special little girl voice for him and said she could see him at his place at four.

It took her twenty minutes to fix her hair into the two braided pig-tails, and then she got out the white blouse, her school blazer, the blue skirt and the flat lace-up shoes. She was only eighteen but he liked to think she was only fourteen and still a schoolgirl. She put on her blue beret and locked the door of her room.

Inspector Schiller lived in a new block of luxury apartments off Kantstrasse. He wasn't a client in the normal sense, although he'd been having sex with her for a year. When she first met him he had been in charge of the Vice Squad that covered the Kurfürstendamm area. Now he was something to do with anti-terrorist things. He was a big burly man and several people said that he looked like Hermann Goering. When he opened the door to her he looked solemn and serious but as soon as the door was closed he was laughing and patting her bottom.

An hour later he lay beside her breathless and gasping

from his efforts. She sat beside him on the bed, her hand on his meaty thigh, waiting for him to recover.

'I'm getting too old for this game, Heidi,' he panted.

'Don't be silly, Max. You're fantastic.'

'How's things at the club?'

'Not bad ... ' She fluttered her eye-lashes. ' ... I've been thinking of leaving.'

'You'd make more as a free-lance, kid. Once you've got the word round.'

'I'm thinking of going to London.'

'Big stuff, eh. How're you going to get a work permit?'

'I'm thinking of getting married.'

The disbelief on his face angered her, and his words angered her more.

'The military wouldn't let a soldier marry a whore.'

'He's not a soldier. And I'm not a whore.'

'Who is he?'

'He's an Englishman.'

'What's his name?'

'Arthur Lowrey.'

'Is he well off?'

'No. But he will be in a few days.'

'Sounds like a con man to me.'

'He's a friend of Charlie's.'

Schiller laughed. 'Birds of a feather. Charlie owes more every month.'

She looked at him intently. 'D'you mean that? Is it true?'

'Of course it is. He borrowed his money to start, from the sharks. They could close him down tomorrow and he wouldn't own the suit he stands up in.'

'You're trying to frighten me, Max.'

'Why the hell should I? Ask Hellman next time he screws you. Ask Lutz.'

'But this guy's not making his money from the club.'

'How's he making it then?'

'He's got something on some politician. He's going to pay him off.'

'A politician in Berlin?'

'Yes.'

He laughed. 'There isn't one of them that's got two pfennigs to rub together.'

'He's East German.'

Schiller sat up slowly, his big hand reached for a cigar from the bedside table. Careful not to look at her as he spoke, he said, 'They're just as broke as our lot. Who is he?'

'I don't know. But he's a Minister.'

Schiller carefully examined the blue smoke as it curled upwards.

'Find out his name and I'll let you know if this fellow's conning you.'

'Oh Max. You're a sweetie. You really are.'

She leaned over and kissed him, and whispered, 'Do you want to have me again?'

'There's a big difference between wanting to and being able to. I'm too old for seconds, my pet.'

She laughed softly. 'I'll let you sleep in peace.'

He watched as she dressed and when she stood at the door he said casually, 'Let me have that chap's name. I'll be out of town for a bit after Thursday.'

'Can I ring you at the office, or must it be here?'

'Either place. It doesn't matter. Just say his name.'

Otto Becker had not had a call for two days but he hadn't left the house in the evenings in case he missed it.

When the door-bell rang just before eight, he almost decided to ignore it. He daren't be away from the phone. Whoever it was he'd get rid of them quickly. And he would hear the phone even at the door.

The man was wearing a heavy, dark blue coat and a hat. He was smiling as he stood there.

'Evening, Erich. I thought I'd pay you a call.'

Becker was aware that his hand was trembling as he held the door.

'Who *are* you?'

'Doesn't matter who *I* am. It's more important who *you* are.'

Becker stood to one side. 'You'd better come in.'

'Are you alone?'

'Yes.'

'Don't try any tricks, mister. If I'm not back tonight that stuff will be delivered by hand tomorrow morning.'

Becker didn't reply, and the man came in, following Becker into the big living-room. Becker pointed to an armchair, and after looking around the room the man sat down. He sat looking at Becker for several minutes before he spoke.

'Have you got the money together?'

'It's going to take me at least another week.'

'I'll give you four days. No more. I've waited long enough.'

'We're not funded until the fifteenth of each month.'

'That's your problem.'

Becker remembered what SIS had told him. To describe the difficulties of getting negotiable cash.

'The dollars are going to be almost impossible.'

'That's your problem too.'

'Would you accept an alternative?'

'Like what?'

'Krugerrands or sovereigns.'

The brown eyes looked intently at Becker's face. Trying to find some clue.

'They'd be too heavy.'

'They're much less bulk unless I can get big denomination notes. And gold coin isn't traceable.'

The man smiled. 'Sounds like you're trying hard, mister. I'll accept either.'

'Where did you get those documents?'

Laughing, the man stood up. 'I'll phone you tomorrow. I'll want something to report to my partners.'

'There's more than you?'

'Of course. If you touch me the others will send off the stuff.'

Laufer looked back and waved as he closed the garden gate. Becker stood silhouetted in the open doorway.

The girl phoned Inspector Schiller at eight the next morning. He reached for a pen to note down the name. But when he heard it he laid the pen down.

'Are you sure, Heidi? Quite sure?'

'That's the name he said, Max.'

'Did he say what he'd got on him?'

'Not really. It was something to do with the war.'

'OK. I'll see what I can find out. Be good.'

She blew him a kiss down the phone and hung up.

Inspector Schiller picked up the red phone and asked for Becker's file. While he was waiting he rang his opposite number in Bonn. Inspector Schiller had been a policeman all his life and his instinct told him that he was on to something. It might end up as no more than a sly dig on 'The Voice of America', but it could well be more.

Gisella Harting lay on her bed in the Rossiya Hotel. She could hear the chimes from the clock in Red Square. She was shivering as if she had a fever. She lay on her side, her knees drawn up, her arms round her legs. It was dark in her room except for the light from the window. The chambermaid had told her that it was the reflection in the sky from the Kremlin floodlights.

She had been utterly exhausted by the flight from Berlin and the scenes at the prison and the hotel. But Chukovsky had insisted on showing her the sights of Moscow. She had been treated like a VIP, champagne on the plane, the suite in the hotel. Cars, bowing and scraping, and not a moment's privacy until now.

Despite her protests they had said that Szabo would have to be transferred to Moscow before he could be released. Polite but formal. And Boris Chukovsky had taken her himself to release Istvan Szabo from his cell in the Lubyanka. The sight of that grim pile just as it had always looked in the press photographs had frightened her. And the stench in the corridors. Urine, vomit, sweat, and fear. As acrid a smell as in the lion house at the zoo.

He was so delighted to see her, and they had been driven back, alone and happy, to her suite at the hotel. All day they had been together, talking and planning. Boris Chukovsky had joined them after lunch. He had arranged all the formalities for their wedding the next day, and they were discussing the possibility of an apartment after they came back from their honeymoon. Then came the knocking on the door. The two uniformed men bursting in, their guns pointing at Istvan. The argument between Chukovsky and the men. Istvan reaching for the telephone and the man's huge fist smashing into his face. They carried him away unconscious.

Chukovsky had phoned somebody. He had spoken in Russian so she couldn't understand what he was saying. But she could tell that he was angry. It was to no avail. He had sighed, and told her how much everyone regretted what had happened, especially in front of her. That part had been done in error. But maybe it was best that she had witnessed the scene. Istvan Szabo, as he had said before, was not treated as she was, and it seemed that their suspicions had been well-founded. They had proof now that Szabo had been selling her information to another intelligence service. Thank God she was not already married to him. It would have put even her position in jeopardy. Meantime she must rest under doctor's orders and recover from the ordeal. Szabo would receive a heavy sentence from the courts and she must forget him. When she was settled in Moscow with a suitable job there would be plenty of sincere Soviets who would appreciate her loyalty and courage.

Hour after hour, as she lay on the bed, her mind had been a battle-field. There was something terribly wrong. She was not convinced by Chukovsky. But what was the something that was wrong. Once, when her mind was almost unhinged she came near the truth and cried out, her head in her hands. It was then that the maid had come in. She spoke German and tried to comfort her. Her suspicious mind thought for a moment that the maid was a jailer rather than a servant. And perhaps a nurse rather than a maid. But an overpowering fear made her realize subconsciously that she must go on believing, or seeming to believe, or her own life might be at risk.

SIS Hamburg had come back with the news that Karl Laufer had been employed in some capacity at two or three clubs on the Reeperbahn which even the tolerant St Pauli police had found obnoxious. It was thought that he had been involved in a series of robberies and had gone to West Berlin with his share of the proceeds. It was not thought that his share would amount to much more than a few thousand Deutschmarks. There were no further entries on his card.

Miller put an SIS man onto the OC of the Military Police detachment in Spandau, who in turn checked with the Berlin police for the whereabouts of a suspect named Laufer. There had been no problem and they had traced Laufer's file on the spot. He had served a short prison sentence on a technicality concerning the use of the hotel next to his club, and was listed as a suspect fence for British and American servicemen who used his club and sold War Department property on the black market. All Miller needed was the address.

He sent a signed note to Richter through one of the SIS contacts in East Berlin. It was merely to boost his morale and let him see that things were happening. He realized what

Richter's state of mind must be: uncertain, fearing every phone call, scared of being exposed, and most of all half-paralysed by the fear of being in the hands of the KGB. Richter had no experience of field-work. He was like Parsons, a desk man, an administrator. He could order assassination or torture, imprisonment or kidnapping, but he was never physically involved. He didn't have to see the fear on men's faces in that second when they knew that they were going to die. He didn't hear the screams or the snapping of finger joints. He issued orders and read reports. Then sent them for filing. But even this second-hand knowledge would make him more scared. He knew what happened when you were caught out. It would be somebody in Moscow who signed the order that sealed his fate, and his closed file would go in some cabinet in Dzerdzhinski Square.

Miller spent an hour reading Parsons' report on how they had used Richter. He had been found a job with a Military Government detachment in the British Zone and had finally been promoted to the Military Government unit at Hanover as liaison between Military Government and German local government. When the first elections were held in post-war Germany his qualifications were ideal. An efficient German who seemed to know how to handle the British. He had been elected with an enormous majority on a Social Democrat ticket.

London had required no more of him than to keep them continuously informed about German political and government attitudes from the inside. In their negotiations, the British were able to use this information discreetly and diplomatically to their own advantage. From the moment when Ulbricht and his associates had gone to the Russian Zone, Richter had been groomed and trained to defect to East Germany. Slowly, in public, his views became more and more anti-British and anti-Western. Critical of the occupying forces and Military Government he was seen as an active dissident by the Germans. A man whose independence was real, who forced more and more concessions from the occupying power. Only in the first few days of his defection to East Germany was there a sense of shock, and then it was seen as the obvious and logical outcome of his views.

The East Germans had interrogated him for a month before they were satisfied that his defection was genuine, and by the end of that time they knew they had a real asset, a man who knew not only what the Bonn politicians were up to but what the British attitude was to both West and East Germany. He was an ally beyond price, and his appointment to the Deputy Ministership was only the start of his new career. There were two conferences with the British authorities in Berlin where SIS ensured that Richter was able to negotiate highly favourable terms for the East Berlin government. His reports to the British on the formation of the Warsaw Pact, the East German politicians and the armed forces were invaluable, but London used him only for information. They never risked using his position of Deputy Minister in charge of the East German Security Services in any practical way. If SIS agents were caught he was not expected to protect them. He reported on the situation but no more. It was a classic use of a penetration operation. Sophisticated and successful, and apparently secure. Only some totally unpredictable event could endanger it. And that was what they had got. If it had been up to him Miller would have got Richter out right away and to hell with embarrassing the Soviets over Gisella Harting.

Fourteen

Miller paid the twenty mark entrance fee and the smiling girl led him to a table. A few moments later she came back with the club's free welcoming drink. Lemon with a vague trace of vodka that went under the name of a Molotov Cocktail.

He looked around slowly and carefully. It was typical of a hundred such clubs around the world where thieves came to negotiate with fences, men came for pretty girls, and, he had to admit, where intelligence men talked to informers.

The pianist was good. Pianists in German clubs nearly always were good. He was playing 'Getting Sentimental Over You' and the Dorsey brothers wouldn't have been ashamed of him. But nobody else appeared to be listening. There were tables for four and tables for two. The foursomes all consisted of two men and two hostesses. The drinks came frequently and the girls' eyes were full of promise. At the tables for two it was always two men. Deep in discussion that seemed sometimes to be angry or hurt as some professional indicated outrage at a fence's offer. At these tables the drink was real, and by the bottle. And the bottles were always Scotch.

He saw the shadow fall across his table and looked up. He recognized the man immediately. It was Karl Laufer. He answered the description perfectly. He was smiling as he leaned forward, one hand on the table and one on the back of Miller's chair. 'Welcome to Club Vogel, sir. Are they looking after you?'

Miller smiled back, amiably. 'They're doing fine. I like the pianist. He's very good.'

'He was studying at Munich for three years, intending to be a concert pianist, and decided he could make more money this way.'

'I hope he does.' Miller smiled.

Laufer nodded. 'He makes more than the mayor of Berlin, I might say.'

Laufer beckoned to one of the girls. 'Another house drink for my friend here.' He turned to look at Miller. 'Are you staying long in Berlin?'

'A couple of weeks I expect.'

'I hope we'll see a lot of you. What d'you think of our girls?'

'They're beautiful. You've got a good eye for girls, Herr ... ?'

'Laufer. Karl Laufer at your service. Would you like a little feminine company? I think they're all hoping to be lucky with you.'

Miller looked around slowly and carefully.

'How about the young blonde with the pony tail. Does she speak English?'

'That's Karen. They all speak English. English, French, and of course, German. And, although we're very very discreet here, we're free and easy too. If you want some private time with one of the girls there's accommodation available next door. You can hire a room or a suite by the hour or for the night. The girl can fix it. They would all welcome the chance of entertaining you.'

'Sounds great. How long have you had the club, Herr Laufer?'

'Oh, several years now. Let me tell Karen to join you.'

Laufer walked across the room and spoke to the girl and

she came over straight away, smiling as she sat down opposite him at the table.

'Hi,' she said. 'Are you American?'

'Why American?'

'You're tanned. You dress like an American, and you look a bit like Cary Grant.'

'D'you like Cary Grant?'

She grinned. 'You bet. And I like men who look like him too.'

And it was at that moment that he saw Lowrey. He was talking to the cigarette girl. Miller turned to the girl at his table. 'What would you like to drink?'

'I'm only allowed to drink champagne.' She smiled.

'I guess they've got to make a buck or two along the way. Can you signal one of the girls?'

She turned, blocking Miller from Lowrey's view. When the drinks came she sipped her champagne and he drank the watered-down whisky, keeping well away from the table-light. He saw Lowrey glare at the cigarette girl, say something and then walk off in obvious anger.

'Looks like the cigarette girl's having a row with a customer.'

The girl turned to look and then turned back again.

'That's Heidi and her new boyfriend. D'you fancy her? She's available.'

'Thanks, honey. Present company's fine for me.'

'Karl said you asked for me. Did you?'

'Yes.'

'Why?'

'Because you're beautiful.'

'D'you want to take me to the hotel?'

'How about you?'

'It's what I'm here for.'

'How much is it?'

'Fifty marks for me and ten for the room. An hour.'

'Let's go then, honey.'

'I'll go first. You pay your bill and they'll give you a key. You have to go out of the club, turn left and it's the second door along. It's painted yellow, there's no name or number. I'll be waiting for you.'

'OK. See you.'

The reception area of the hotel consisted of a small hallway with a single desk. An old man sat at the desk, an old-fashioned pair of wooden crutches alongside him on the floor. And despite the law, he wore an Iron Cross defiantly on his jacket. But nobody was going to prosecute an ex-service man with leather stumps instead of legs. Miller gave him ten marks and slid two coins in the saucer on the desk.

'Heil Hitler,' the old man said, and he wasn't joking. 'You're in number seven. The bell will ring when your time's up.'

The girl was waiting for him at the top of the stairs. She had taken off the white briefs and her naked body glowed in the soft red lighting.

The room was small but clean. The walls white, and hung with mildly erotic drawings. He gave her the fifty marks and she lay on the bed watching as he undressed.

As he lay naked beside her he was aware that she was the first girl he had slept with apart from his wife since the day he was married. It somehow seemed fitting that she should be a Berlin whore. But he knew that that was only special pleading. She was young and pretty, her body utterly desirable, and he wanted her just as much as the others who used her.

Half an hour later, she had stretched out and switched on the music.

'If you're hungry we can send for a meal from the club. We've still got twenty minutes.' She smiled. 'It's fast service and the food's not bad.'

'How about we book another hour and then order the food?'

'Are you United States Navy?'

'No. Why?'

'I thought only sailors wanted more than an hour.'

He smiled. 'Sailors and dirty old men.'

'You're not old, honey, and if wanting to sleep with a girl is dirty, then all men are dirty.'

He gave her a hundred marks. 'You see to it, sweetie.'

She phoned down to the old man at reception and then turned back to look at him.

'How long are you in Berlin?'

'A couple of weeks.'

'Do you know Berlin?'

'I was here after the war and I've been here a couple of times since.'

'What do you do. What's your job?'

'What do you think it is?'

She looked at his face. 'Something outdoors. Something tough. You're very strong. You notice everything but you're kind of closed in. You could be FBI or the Mafia. If you were Italian I'd bet money on *Cosa Nostra* .'

He smiled. 'I'm a writer. I'm doing research in Berlin for a novel.'

She smiled disbelievingly. 'OK. You're a writer. The customer's always right.'

The meal wasn't too bad and as they finished off the bottle of wine he said, 'What's Laufer like as a boss?'

'Much the same as all of them. Charming on the outside, a bastard in private.'

'Does he sleep with the girls?'

'Of course he does.'

'Have you got a steady boyfriend?'

'No. A boyfriend wouldn't let me work here. He'd be jealous. I've tried it. And if he'd let me do this I wouldn't want him.'

'You said the cigarette girl was talking to her boyfriend.'

'Oh him. He's an old friend of Karl's. They're doing some deal together.'

'What's his name?'

She looked at him. 'You're not a writer are you? Are you a hit man?'

'No.'

'Then what are you?'

He reached for his wallet and took out two fifty mark notes and gave them to her.

'Like I said. I'm doing research. What's his name?'

'Lowrey. Arthur Lowrey. He's English.'

'Where does he live?'

'He's got a room at a *pension* somewhere. I don't know where. But he spends most of his time here at the club. He sleeps in the hotel some nights. With Heidi.'

'Are you friends with Heidi?'

'Yes.'

'How long before the club closes?'

'What time is it now?'

'One o'clock.'

'There's another four hours to closing time.'

He gave her another hundred marks. 'I'll wait up here for you. Go down now and find out where his room is.'

Her blue eyes looked back at him. 'You're some sort of cop aren't you?' And she was scared by the cold look in his eyes. She got up off the bed and pulled her panties up her long legs.

'I'll be waiting for you, honey,' he said.

As she stood at the door she said, 'When you screwed me I'd have sworn that you really wanted me. It was just a cover wasn't it?'

He reached out for her and his hand went up between her legs as he looked up at her face. 'If it was a cover, I needn't have actually done it. And I'll do it again now if you don't believe me.'

She shrugged and laughed softly. 'I'll be back in a few minutes.'

It was a quarter of an hour before she came back and as she took off her pants and lay on the bed beside him she kissed him and said, 'Pension Allgau, it's not far from Check-point Charlie.'

She had given him the telephone number of her apartment when he left the hotel just after seven o'clock the next morning. There was snow on the sidewalks as he twisted and turned through the back streets, but nobody had followed him. He hailed a taxi near the Gedächtnis Kirche, its blue lights eerie in the early morning darkness, and it dropped him at the corner of the safe-house road. The drivers probably knew that it was an SIS house but the operators always stuck to the standard routine from habit.

Parsons was waiting for him. He had flown in after leaving Thurston in charge of the London end. There was little to cover from London now that couldn't be handled by phone or radio. It was in Berlin that Miller would need help. Arrangements were made for a twenty-four-hour surveillance on Lowrey and Laufer, and that would take sixteen men and two women from SIS's Berlin resources.

An experienced operator had been sent to book in at the Pension Allgau and Lowrey had not yet returned to his room from the club.

Lowrey's room had been expertly searched, and a photocopy of the two documents had been found and photographed. It didn't need an expert to find them, they were in a drawer under two nylon shirts and a pair of Marks and Spencer's pants. The room had been photographed from a dozen angles for the record.

Miller stood looking at the wet prints as soon as they had been fixed. He remembered both letters. The earlier one was his original orders from Mayne to operate Richter back against the Abwehr and confirmed his change of status from prisoner to collaborator. Collaborator was the formal and official description for 'turned' agents in those days. In today's terminology it would be utterly damning. The second letter was to him from Mayne confirming that Richter would be financially rewarded, given a complete new background and identity, with supporting documents. And the final instruction in that letter ordered him to be responsible for the destruction of all SIS files and documentation relating to Richter and his operation. His own rather juvenile initials were alongside the date-received stamp. Both letters were headed, 'Eyes only D. Miller Intelligence Corps, 10350556'. The first one showed his rank as captain, the second as major. What puzzled him was why, all those years ago, a man like Lowrey should have kept those two letters. He couldn't possibly have been far-sighted enough to know that years later they could be worth money. Nobody could have known that. Richter had gone back to Germany with false papers but there were tens of thousands of Germans who had taken the opportunity of changing identities in the utter chaos of post-war Germany. Men escaping from wives and families, war criminals, men whose arrest would be automatic, they all had more to fear from exposure than Richter. Even Mayne himself, or his successors in controlling Richter, could never have guessed that his political career would be so successful. Nothing had been fiddled, no direct or indirect pressures had been applied, Richter had succeeded mainly on his own account. His knowledge, his ability to parley with the British Military Government, only worked once he was a civil servant and politician. And nobody could have known that he would achieve that status. And both Lowrey and Laufer looked typical Soho spivs. Laufer a shade more sophisticated than Lowrey, but there wasn't much in it. What possible reason could Lowrey have had for stealing those two letters? But the problem now was to find the originals before they could be used. Even the photocopies could do irrevocable damage to Richter's position, but at least doubt could be thrown on their authenticity. The originals would be utterly damning. The KGB wouldn't want proof. The vaguest suspicion would be enough, and Richter would be dead or on a plane for Moscow in an hour.

Miller asked for a manipulated passport. A genuine passport with the only spurious item his own photograph. The passport had a three-month East German visa with six weeks still to run. His occupation was given as 'Importer – precision instruments'.

He had gone through Check-point Charlie without problems and had headed for Unter den Linden. Three times he had walked the length of the broad avenue, the last time crossing over at the far end to the Soviet Embassy, standing, watching and waiting patiently. The snow was settling fast as he crossed back and walked down the north side. On the far side of the avenue he saw the lights go out in the shop. He walked almost to the Brandenburger Tor before he crossed and walked back up the south side. Slowing down as he approached the shop.

At first he didn't see them and he had broken the rules by stopping to look. The two paperbacks stood side by side. Karl Marx's *Correspondenz zwischen Marx-Engels und Lasalle* and Engels' *Briefe an Margaret Harkness und Mischa Kautsky*. He walked to the door and gave the signal on the bell.

It was the old man's daughter who answered and opened the door. She was seventeen. The old man was only forty-five, but three years in Dachau had left marks beyond the tattoo on his arm. The girl looked a typical pretty Nordic blonde. But she wasn't. She was in fact a typical dark-haired Pole. It just made life easier to look like a typical German blonde. Her father's bookshop was an SIS dead-letter drop, and once or twice a year he sent radio messages back to London when there was a real emergency.

The girl said softly, '*Kto idzie do lasu?*' And he replied,

'*Nikt, nie mamy czasu.*' She stood aside to let him in, and he waited as she locked the door. She pointed to the stairs and he went up slowly. He didn't like walking up stairs in strange places. Especially when they were steep and there was a half-open door at the top.

He stood motionless outside the door, holding his breath as his hand reached forward and pushed the door back until it was flat against the inner wall. His other hand was around the gun in his pocket.

Richter was sitting there, alone, with a glass in one hand, and a cigar in the other, as it rested on the arm of his chair, trembling slightly.

Miller walked slowly into the room and Richter saw him. He stood up clumsily from the chair, spilling his drink as he stumbled forward, his arms outstretched to embrace his old friend. They stood looking at each other for long moments, and then Richter said, 'It's been a long long time, my friend.'

Miller gave the German's arm a friendly squeeze. 'Let's sit down and talk. We haven't much time. Did they contact you today?'

'Not yet. It's always at eight o'clock.'

'I think I've traced them. There's two of them. Both amateurs.'

'Have they been picked up yet?'

'I can't do that, Erich. I need to get my hands on the originals and find out if there are more copies, and if there are more people involved.'

'The one who came to my house looked no more than a petty crook.'

'He is.'

'So what next?'

'They're under constant surveillance now. But I must know much more before we pull them in. I can't take the risk of there being a third, or some system that sends off the documents as soon as they are arrested. It will take me some days.'

'I am anxious, David. Scared.'

'So should I be. How long before Khrushchev's visit?'

'Five more days. But these things are sometimes put back or brought forward for security reasons.'

'If it's altered, treat it as an emergency, contact the old man.'

'What if they pressure me, threaten me again?'

'If you think you can't stall them, tell the old man to contact me immediately. If I can't deal with it over here I'll come straight in for you.'

'You are sure you can get me out?'

'No doubt at all, Erich.' Miller stood up. 'I'll go first. You leave a couple of minutes later, and I'll check that you're not being followed.'

From the other side of the street Miller watched Richter leave, and then waited until he turned the corner at the far end. Nobody followed him. He moved into the darkness of a shop doorway and shifted the gun from his pocket back to the holster under his left arm.

There were few people on the streets and the snow was drifting down quietly and relentlessly. He was held up for ten minutes at the check-point, while the guard phoned some central office to check the validity of his visa. It was merely a random check that they carried out on visas several times a day.

The surveillance reports came in hourly and he sat reading them in his room. Lowrey was still at Club Vogel and for most of the time he had been closeted with Laufer in his office. The only other identifiable customers were a US Senator who had two of the girls at his table and a Japanese who was Berlin representative of a Tokyo hi-fi manufacturer. He had brought his own girl. There was a junior but middle-aged officer from the West German security police in mufti and complete with hostess, and a party of four, a BBC TV team doing a documentary on the Wall.

Miller listened to the midnight radio bulletin on RIAS-Berlin as he undressed. The Christine Keeler case was still grinding on. The Beatles had been presented with a golden disc, and a court in New York had allowed the publication of *Fanny Hill*. Restrictions at the Wall check-points were being rigidly applied and there was more snow to come. He switched off the radio, phoned the duty officer for a 6 am call, and pulled the blankets over his shoulders. Then he noticed the two letters on his bedside table as he reached to switch out the lamp. They were both addressed to his accommodation address where letters were routed to the Foreign Office and then on to him, wherever he happened to be.

He opened the thick one first. It was a petition for divorce with a brief covering letter from a solicitor in Maidenhead. The petition cited continual neglect of wife and child, mental cruelty, and constructive desertion. The case was down for hearing on 21 February 1964. Alimony was claimed, pending the hearing, of £75 a month for the wife and £30 a month for the child, excluding a claim for fees for the child's further education.

The second letter was advance notification that when the present operation was over he was granted twenty-one days' leave and would then be officially transferred to the Foreign Office establishment as liaison officer between SIS and the FO Intelligence Committee. His upgrading would be backdated to 23 November when he had been withdrawn as CIA/SIS liaison.

He put both letters back in their envelopes, switched off the bedside light, closed his eyes, and slept.

Fifteen

He was eating his breakfast when the orderly put the slip on the table beside his plate. A message had come through from London, giving a London telephone number and asking him to ring it as a matter of urgency. It was not a number he recognized. Standing up, he drank the last of his tea as he walked through to the radio room. He gave the number to the signals corporal and walked over to one of the plastic enclosures. A couple of minutes later the call came through.

'Miller.'

'Is that you, daddy?'

'Yes. Is that Penny Ann?'

'Yes.'

'What can I do for you?'

'It's nice to hear a calm, sane voice at last.'

'Why. What's the matter?'

There was a pause before she answered.

'I'm preggers, daddy. Three months' worth.'

'Who's the lucky man?'

'I'm afraid he's somebody else's husband.'

'D'you love him?'

'Yes. I'm afraid I do.'

'Does he love you?'

'I don't think so. And he's financially dependent on his wife. There's no question of him leaving her.'

'Is that why you're upset?'

'Not really.'

'Tell me.'

'I want to have the baby.'

'Go on.'

'They won't let me. They say I've got to have a quiet abortion.'

'Who's *they?*'

'Grandmother mainly.'

'What does your mother say?'

'She can't make up her mind. The usual pressures from grandma about neighbours, reputations, scandals, no prospects of marriage for an unmarried mother. And Peter's gone a bit withdrawn on her . . . '

'That's bullshit, girl. It's your decision not theirs.'

'I know, but I won't survive without their financial help.'

'Of course you will. I'll support you financially and every other way. I'll be back in London permanently in a few weeks' time. We'll find a place for both of us. Meantime I'll instruct the bank to pay you sixty a month. Is that enough?'

'It's too much.'

'Well that settles that. What's your present address?'

'57 Abinger Road, Chiswick.'

'I'll do that right now. And one more thing.'

'What's that?'

'Just sit down, somewhere nice. In the park. In peace. Think it out. Ignore their comments, but think it through. And whatever you decide I'll support. Nothing but what *you* want matters. And one more thing . . . '

'What?'

'I love you, and I'll love your baby too. So don't worry.'

'And I love *you* . And thanks.'

'OK then?'

'Yes. How are you?'

'Surviving, as usual.'

'Take care.'

'OK. And you.'

As he hung up he checked in his notebook and asked the duty corporal to get his bank. Ten minutes later it was all fixed.

He was glad that she had phoned him, and angry at the pressures put on her. Their solution had some validity, but their arguments and pressures were despicable, and would only make her more determined to go her own way. Despite her outward coolness and calm she had always been a warm, loving creature. And at nineteen she would be very vulnerable. Stunningly pretty, young and vital, there would be dozens of suitors and would-be lovers. He wondered what the man was like. He ought to hate him, but he didn't. Penny Ann wouldn't have succumbed to the first Lothario who came along.

Back in his office he read the reports on his desk.

Lowrey had stayed all night with the cigarette girl. Her name was Heidi Lemke, and they'd stayed at the hotel next to Club Vogel. Room Ten. Laufer had left the club for an hour, mid-evening, and had taken a taxi to the Hilton. He'd been to room 4251 which was occupied by a US Army Captain. They had interviewed him later. He had bought 7,000 US dollars' worth of jewellery and watches from Laufer. They had left him with his goods although it was obvious that he knew that the stuff had been stolen.

Only the last report worried Miller. A man named Schiller, who.had told the landlady that he was a police inspector, had gone to the Pension Allgau. After demanding the key to Lowrey's room, he had been in there an hour. He appeared to have taken nothing, and had asked no questions of the proprietor when he handed back the key.

Miller phoned through to Central Registry to see if there

was a file or a card on a police inspector named Schiller. It came back almost immediately and Miller didn't like what he read. Inspector Otto Schiller was in charge of the West Berlin police unit responsible for counter-espionage – far too senior to be doing a routine search of a hotel room. He must know something, and it meant another set of people keeping surveillance on Laufer and Lowrey. He remembered the list of identified customers at the Club Vogel. One of them had been one of Schiller's men, so they were probably covering Laufer too. Even if they had only been covering Lowrey at first they would have picked up the connection with Laufer sooner or later.

Schiller phoned his opposite number in Bonn and two hours later he received orders to fly down to the capital immediately. As the landing gear came down, Schiller looked out across the dark landscape. He had always hated the airfield at Wahn. It reminded him of Russia and the flat, deserted heaths and the grim, black pine forests. That day, as if to make the point, the ground was covered with snow.

There was a black Ministry Mercedes waiting for him at the terminal entrance, and Steinitz put a warning finger to his lips as the driver closed the rear door.

They talked about football and families until they got to the white façaded government block. As they walked up the steps together to the main entrance, Steinitz said, 'We're going straight in to see Oetker. He's Deputy Foreign Minister and very interested. Becker was a colleague of his in his days at Hanover.'

They were kept waiting in the outer office for about ten minutes before being ushered into Deputy Minister Oetker. He waved them both to the chairs facing his desk. He nodded towards Steinitz and then looked at Schiller.

'Tell me what you know so far, Herr Inspector.'

Schiller cleared his throat. 'I received information that an

149

Englishman named Lowrey, staying in Berlin, was expecting to make money by blackmailing Deputy Minister Becker.'

'On what grounds?'

'I don't really know. It was in very general terms. All my informant could say was that it was something to do with the war.'

Oetker turned to look at Steinitz.

'What have we got on Becker's war service in our records?'

'Nothing before June 1945. Absolutely nothing. A blank.'

'Where was he born?'

'On our records it's Dresden, but that may not be true. There is no way of checking.'

'There'll be nothing left there. All their records went in the bombing that night. And if there *were* any records they wouldn't pass them to us now.'

A secretary knocked and came in, and he waved her away.

'Does it give no details of his war service in the files?'

'Just his discharge papers.'

'What do they say?'

'Practically nothing. Just, "Discharged German Army from British PW camp, August 1945" and the Barleycorn stamp.'

'What's a Barleycorn stamp?'

'It was the British code-word for an operation in 1945 to release privates and NCOs to work on the land, to get the harvest in. Mil. Gov. were scared about the shortage of food.'

'What kind of people did they release?'

'Just other ranks. Wehrmacht and Navy.'

'Were they screened by the British before they were released?'

'Yes, but it was pretty rough and ready. They weren't all that interested in service people.'

'But at least that establishes that he served in the Wehrmacht, and that he wasn't an officer.'

'Yes.'

'So what can he have done in war-time that allows these people to blackmail him?'

'Rape? Murder? Black market?'

Oetker's eyebrows went up. 'Black market? There wouldn't be a Cabinet Minister left on either side if that was blackmail material. Anybody alive today owes it in some way or other to the black market and rape. Find me a woman who was in Berlin when the Red Army came in who wasn't raped. I suppose it could be murder. But Becker never struck me as the type for murder.'

'They never do look like murderers, Herr Deputy Minister,' said Schiller.

'I suppose not. Is there anything I can do to help?'

'Would the British help? They might have records on discharged prisoners of war.'

Oetker nodded. 'I'll see what I can find out.'

'Do we have anyone in East Berlin who could have a look at the records there?' Steinitz asked.

'I'll see.'

'And maybe the British could supply something on Lowrey. I should think he'd have a record.'

'I can but try. Well, gentlemen,' he said, standing up, 'thank you for your valuable time. Keep on with it, but it's not a matter for top priority. Of course if we got something to embarrass the East we'd be delighted.'

He shook hands with both men and then reached for his telephone as they left.

On the way back to the car, Schiller said, 'D'you reckon he'll do anything?'

'You bet he will. All that cool was a front.'

The old woman sat in her usual chair, her hands crossed over her stomach. Her husband hovered behind her, tentatively touching a book here and there on the shelves, moving an ornament on the mantelpiece, trying not to be involved. Penny sat on the embroidered stool and her new man, Peter, sat to one side in one of the armchairs.

The old woman shook her head irritably as she spoke.

'You can't possibly allow it, Penny. We discussed it fully. All of us. It was decided then and, reluctantly, I might say, I agreed to pay for it to be done.'

'I'm afraid Penny Ann didn't agree.'

'But she was here.'

'I know. But she didn't agree then, and she doesn't agree now.'

'She's *got* to agree. All of us are involved. What explanation do you imagine we can give to people?'

'She doesn't intend to live here.'

'And where, pray, does she intend to live?'

'In London. She has an offer already.'

'I can well imagine what kind of offer nineteen-year-old girls with babies will get.'

'She'll be living with her father.'

Anger and disbelief fought on the old woman's face. For long moments she was literally speechless.

'That man. That terrible man. You must forbid it.'

'I'm in no position to forbid it.'

'Make her a Ward of Court. Or I will. She needs some sense knocking into her stupid head.'

'She's not stupid, mother. She just sees things differently. That's all. It will be her baby.'

'Baby. I ask you. Peter,' she turned to the man, 'can't you get some sense into my daughter's head? Just think of *your* job and *your* relatives and friends.'

Peter Lawson looked at the pattern on his brogues before turning towards his future wife.

'I don't want to insist, Penny. But it *is* going to mean problems.'

'What problems?'

He shrugged. 'Explanations, lies, all the sort of things that go with this sort of situation.'

'Is that how you'd feel if I had an illegitimate child?'

'Oh come, Penny. That's ridiculous. She won't even tell you who the father is. Surely you're entitled to know that?'

'What difference would it make if we did know his name?'

Peter Lawson shrugged towards the old lady. And then stood up, looking at his watch.

'I'm afraid I'm on call tomorrow so I'll have to be popping along. How about a quick one at the Feathers, old girl?'

She looked up at his face and slowly shook her head. The words 'old girl' tolled like a funeral bell in her mind. She tried to imagine David calling her 'old girl', and suddenly she wanted to cry.

As the door closed behind Peter Lawson the old lady leaned forward.

'Now you just listen, my girl. You will make Penny Ann a Ward of Court tomorrow, or I will. There's going to be no more messing about.'

She looked up, sighing. 'And what good will that do?'

'The court can decide about the child. And that will be that.'

'They can't stop it being born.'

'More's the pity. But they *can* decide what happens to it afterwards.'

'You mean against Penny Ann's wishes?'

'If necessary.'

'Say that they decided that it should be taken into care. In a home?'

'So much the better for all of us.'

'I can't believe you really mean that, mother.'

'Don't make any mistake, my girl. I mean it all right.'

'Just think carefully, mother, before you answer. You're saying that against Penny Ann's wishes you would see her child put in a home?'

153

'Exactly.'

'I said think carefully. It's important to me.'

'Don't dictate to me what to do. I've said what I mean and that's all there is to it.'

Penny Miller stood up slowly, feeling slightly giddy, and she was breathing heavily as she looked at her mother.

'David always said you weren't ill, but sick. Mentally sick. He was right. You *are* an evil woman. I'm glad that my daughter has escaped. And now I'm escaping too.' She turned to her father. 'If you let her interfere by going to the courts, this is the last you'll see of me. I'm going back to my house tonight.' She held out her hand. 'You've got my car keys.'

He said uneasily, 'I'll need the car to do the shopping tomorrow morning. It's Friday.'

'Bugger the shopping. It's my car. Give me those keys.'

He fished in his pocket and held out the keys. As she took them her mother's head sank onto her shoulder.

She looked at her father. 'Maybe you'd better ring for an ambulance.'

It took her an hour to stow her things into the MG but it calmed her down. She drove back to her home with the car hood down despite the cold. She heard the words again and again. The words that were meant to decide her daughter's happiness. They would never have dared to say those things if David had still been alive. And then she realized with a rush that he *was* still alive. She had tried to wipe him from her life, and had almost succeeded with the encouragement of her mother and her new man. Man? What a creep. What an 18-carat creep. Penny Ann had said that she had phoned David's London contact number and twenty minutes later he had called her from Berlin. And with no drama, no fuss, he'd made her happy and secure, just as *she* had once been. And what the hell did it matter that he was away so much? Other husbands were away too – sailors, businessmen, soldiers, even film stars. People might comment about those cold grey eyes and the handsome closed-up face, but if he was on your side you'd have nothing to worry about. And David Miller had always been on her side. One hundred per cent. What a fool she'd been to be influenced by other people. But according to Penny Ann he was going to be back for good in two weeks' time. She would phone him and please God he would listen, and still be on her side. She would phone the solicitors in the morning. Maybe they could all be together again for Christmas.

Sixteen

It had always been left for him to phone her when he was overseas. He had never asked for it to be that way, it just happened.

She was surprised when she rang the accommodation number in London that when she said that she was Mrs Miller she was treated as someone of importance. Of course they could put her in touch immediately. If she would hang up for a couple of minutes they would make the connection. It would be quicker and easier that way, he said, they had special post office lines that were free of static.

She wasn't sure whether they had told him who was phoning. His voice was very clear but noncommittal.

'Miller. Who's calling?'

'It's me, Penny.'

'Hi, Penny Ann.'

'It's not Penny Ann, Dave, it's me, Penny.'

'Well, hello. You two sound just the same on the phone.'

'I've got a problem, Dave.'

'I know, but she's got to be allowed to make up her own mind. She's a young woman now, not a child.'

'I agree. But it's me who's got the problem.'

'I'm sorry to hear that. What's the problem?'

'The problem is that I don't know how to apologize for all the trouble I've caused you.'

There was a pause at the other end and she held her breath as she waited for him to speak.

'You don't have to apologize, Penny. You had a lot to put up with because of my job. I didn't like what you did, but I understand. And you've had pressures from other people.'

'What I did was stupid and immature. At least I could have talked it over with you before I took such definite steps.'

'If I'd been around you probably would have talked it over with me.'

'I was just a bloody coward, and I'm terribly sorry.'

'We're all cowards some of the time.'

'You're not.'

'I am sometimes.'

She closed her eyes as she spoke. 'Would you have me back?'

She was going to count the seconds before he replied. But there was no interval. He replied without any hesitation.

'Of course. You know that.'

'What about Peter Lawson?'

'What about him?'

'Will you be able to forgive that part?'

'He was just a symbol, kid. You have to kiss a lot of frogs before you find a prince.'

'Why are you always so calm, and tolerant, and sensible?'

'If I am I guess it's because of my work.'

'Why that?'

'Well, I see a lot of what happens to people. They waste their last hours and days because they don't know that they're going to die. It helps you to realize what's important and what is trivial.'

'I walked out on my parents. There was a terrible row about Penny Ann, and I realized what they were really like. It was as if you were there, listening, and looking at me with your eyebrows raised. Asking me if that was what I really wanted.'

'Where are you staying?'

'I'm back at the house and Penny Ann's with me.'

'Good for you. Take care of one another until I get back.'

'When can I see you, Dave? I miss you so much.'

'I miss you too. I'd say it will take another seven to ten days to clear up what I'm doing here. I've already been posted back to London permanently. I'll be back before Christmas anyway.'

'We'll have a real family Christmas. Tree, decorations, wrapping paper, turkey, the lot.'

'Good girl. If you get any problems just phone that number. They may not always be able to contact me as easily as today. But they'll get a message through. And don't worry about anything. It's all going to be fine.'

'OK. I love you, Dave. I really do.'

She heard him laugh. 'I love you too. Take care, sweetie.'

And she hung up slowly.

Miller looked over the reports from the surveillance team and he knew that it was all taking too long. Something was going to go wrong if he didn't act soon. But he was undecided about what to do. He needed to be in two places at once – on top of Lowrey in West Berlin, and alongside Richter in East Berlin. Experience told him that something always happened at this stage, something that pointed the way. He had to hold on until that something happened, and hope that he would recognize it.

It happened in less than an hour. A warning from signals in London that a call would be coming through for him personally in ten minutes' time. They would be using the variable scrambler that changed the coded voice pattern every few seconds. So far as they knew it was totally secure to Berlin.

He heard the preliminary clicking and buzzing before London spoke.

'David?'

'Speaking.'

'Base 904 here.'

'Go ahead.'

'Bonn have informed our Embassy and the United States Embassy that your particular old friend from RVPS, the shredder man, is under surveillance by West German security. They are aware of blackmail and target, but not of the grounds for blackmail. Do you understand?'

'Yes. Carry on.'

'They mustn't learn grounds. No matter what that takes. Understood?'

'Yes.'

'No restrictions now. Entirely at your discretion.'

'What about the shredder's new partner?'

'At your discretion.'

'And my official friend?'

'Everything now at your discretion. Our use of him must not, repeat not, ever come out. Discuss with "P" and if necessary refer back to us. OK?'

'Yes. OK.'

The clicking and whining came back, and then the line just carried a noise like a rushing wind. He hung up, and sent the duty clerk to find Parsons.

Parsons sat with his elbows on the table, his hands together as if he were praying, his fingers steepled as he tapped them against his teeth. Then he folded his arms on the table, his shoulders hunched as he looked at Miller.

'Let's go back to this bloody woman Gisella Harting. It was Richter who tipped us off that she was sending stuff to the Soviets through a KGB man named Istvan Szabo.

Planning Group Four weren't told what we know. They would have wanted to know who the someone was, and Richter was far too valuable to us to risk breaking his security.

'It's a small group, and they couldn't have gone on behaving normally if they had known who we suspected. We told all concerned that we had reason to believe there were leaks from Group Four. Nobody really believed us but their material was so high-grade that they accepted tighter security and two changes of personnel.

'We formed Planning Group Ten with selected people. Their brief was to exaggerate our supposed reaction to any aggressive moves by Warsaw Pact countries. Their team-leader was told that it was an experiment, but he wasn't told the reason for the experiment. Nobody else was told anything, not even the NATO security people, or any of the governments who had men in the group.

'When Harting actually defected, the Americans were only told that Harting had been under surveillance and that the information she had been passing was spurious. There's going to be a lot of flak on London when the other NATO countries realize what's been going on. But we're happy to ride that if and when it comes.

'The West Germans, who don't know anything about any of it now, think that they've discovered a way to embarrass the East Germans about an East German Minister. They want to find out what Lowrey and Laufer have got on the man they know as Becker and then expose him. We can't let them do that, and we can't afford to let them find out that Richter not only worked for us during the war, but also when he was a West German politician, and since then when he was an East German Deputy Minister.

'The Khrushchev visit doesn't matter all that much now. We've got two straight objectives. Firstly, get Richter out. And secondly, stop the blackmailers from exposing him while he's still there, *and* afterwards.'

'That doesn't leave me any choice, does it?'

'It depends on whether anybody else is involved with Lowrey and Laufer.'

'I'll have to pull them in to find out.'

'You'll have to use the other safe-house. We're too exposed here.'

'And if there is a third man he can expose Richter the moment I pick the other two up.'

'I'm afraid that's your problem.'

'Thanks.'

'There's nothing that anyone else can do. It would mean bringing in another field officer and briefing him on the whole set-up before he could be of any use to you.'

'We haven't got time for that.'

'We'll give you any help we can. But London want the minimum number of people involved.'

'So that there aren't too many bodies if they have to throw us to the wolves.'

'You know this game better than I do, David. And you know the rules.'

'Where's the other safe-house?'

'In Grunewald. It's in the woods. Completely isolated. There's an experienced team there. A small one. But you can take as many as you want from here.'

'I shall want a full radio network until I've got them both. And I'll want two experienced snatch teams.'

'That's OK. Who are you going to pull in first, Lowrey or Laufer?'

'Neither. I want the cigarette girl first. Heidi whatever her name is. I need to find out how much she knows.'

'You couldn't release her until you've got Richter across.'

'I don't intend to.'

Parsons stood up. 'I'll go and collect the two teams, brief them, and lay on the radio net. It'll have to be in clear, there's no time for people to absorb a code.'

Miller nodded, reached for his pad, made some notes, and then walked over to look at the large scale map of Berlin that covered one wall. The safe-house in the woods was marked with a blue pin.

Miller gave his briefing to the teams who would be working for him. They had read the surveillance team's reports and had been given photographs of Laufer, Lowrey, and Heidi Lemke.

One of the local drivers took him to the safe-house in Grunewald. They had come off the highway at Koenigsallee, then on past the lake for a couple of kilometres to a right turn that took them down a cinder track, back towards the lake. The car pulled up in front of a pair of tall, wrought-iron gates that carried the shield of the Berlin city bear.

The driver pressed a button on the dashboard and one of the gates slowly swung open to let them through. The gardens looked well-kept, and the snow had been swept from the wide, macadam drive up to the house.

The house itself was obviously pre-war but extensions had been added on each side which, with its white painted exterior and its four arches along the front, gave it a slightly Spanish appearance. To the right was a separate group of buildings that could once have been stables, but now seemed to be garages. On the roof of the main house a TV aerial sprouted from the chimney and a thin whip aerial extended upwards from the TV aerial. It was painted white and pale blue, and unless you expected it to be there you wouldn't have noticed it, camouflaged against the wintry sky. There were two BMWs and a Ford Taunas parked near the garages, and a motor-cycle rested on its stand under one of the arches along the front of the house.

As they pulled up in front of the house a man walked out to the car and opened his door.

'Hi, David.'

It was 'Sunny' Briers. He had been one of Miller's juniors three years before on a six-month stint in the Lebanon.

'How long have you been in Berlin, Sunny?'

'Nearly a year now. Off and on.'

Miller eased himself out of the car, and they walked together to the open door of the house.

'What facilities have you got here?'

'Same as at the other place.'

'A link with London?'

'Yes.'

'People?'

'Four signals, a photographer, a document guy and eight all-rounders. Parsons is sending people over when you let him know what you want.'

'How many interrogation rooms?'

'Four class one and another four that are less secure.'

'What's your cover?'

'Political evaluation team on detachment from HQ British Forces Berlin.'

'Has Parsons briefed you?'

'Not a word. Just said that we were to drop everything and support you in any way you want.'

'Does that create any problems?'

'Nothing we can't cope with.'

Briers showed him round the house and introduced him to all the staff. An office had been cleared for him with a camp-bed in one corner. He dumped his kit on the bed and turned to look at Briers.

'Where can I brief you?'

'Here. We check for bugs every day. We've never found any in the house or the grounds. A car gets bugged from time to time but that's all.'

There was a card-table covered in green baize and there were four folding chairs. Miller closed his eyes for a moment to sort out what he could say. Then he looked over at Briers.

'I'll be pulling in a girl, Heidi Lemke – a hostess at a night-club. We'll have to hold her until the operation's over. Then two men, one British, one German – Lowrey and Laufer.' He paused for a moment as he looked at Briers' face. 'Have you got disposal facilities if it's necessary?'

'There's hundreds of acres of woods.'

'Nothing more secure than that?'

'I'm afraid not. Disposals are not our line of country.'

Miller got the message of disapproval but wasn't moved by it. That attitude was a luxury he couldn't afford. He understood it, and neither approved nor disapproved. Briers' turn would come.

'I'll look after that then. If it's necessary.'

'No way, David. If it has to be done, we'll do it.'

Miller smiled as he looked at the younger man. He was going to comment, and then changed his mind.

'I'd better contact Parsons.'

'I'll leave you to it. I'm in the second office down the corridor.' Briers nodded towards the far wall. 'There's food and soft drinks in the small fridge over there.'

Miller watched Briers as he walked to the door, trying to remember how old he was. He guessed it was mid-thirties. He wouldn't have had any wartime service. Miller subconsciously classified all men on whether they had, or had not, been in the services during the war. With no particular love of the army himself, he still felt more at home with men who had served in the war. They seemed to him to be more reliable. They may have spent their war in some cushy billet, never seeing any action, but he understood them without thinking. They responded more easily to him too. It was as if the war was still going on behind the scenes, which of course it was. But it was a very different war. No gallantry. Not a war for gentlemen.

He looked round for the phone and saw three on a shelf. He used the one marked 'Direct' and dialled the girl's number. She answered straight away.

'Karen Weismuller.'

'Hi, kid. It's the Mafia man.'

'Who ... oh ... yes. I'm only half awake.'

'Don't worry. Are you going to be at the club tonight?'

'Of course.'

'I'll see you there, but I want something right now.'

She laughed softly. 'That's one thing you can't do on the phone, honey. But I'm sure the Bundes Post are working on it.'

'OK, OK. You win. Listen, I want Heidi Lemke's home address and her telephone number. Have you got it handy?'

'Why do you want it?'

'Several reasons.'

'Tell me one.'

'She's got lovely long legs.'

'Tell me another.'

'I want to talk to her.'

'About her boyfriend?'

'Maybe.'

'She's going to marry him you know. It's all settled.'

'She'd be very silly to do that.'

'Somebody else told her that.'

'Who?'

'One of her clients.'

'What did he say?'

'He said Lowrey was a con-man and a crook.'

'Maybe he's a crook with a heart of gold.'

'Is he a crook?'

'How about you leave it to me to tell her what's wrong.'

'You are a cop aren't you?'

'What's her address, sweetie?'

'Hold on. I'll check in my book.'

She was back a few seconds later.

'D'you know the Europa Centre?'

'Yes.'

'She's got a room at the back of a small art gallery there. It's called Gemäldegalerie Kokoshka. There's no phone but the gallery will take messages, but not for business, the gallery owner doesn't approve.'

'Thanks, kid. See you tonight.'

'D'you want me for tonight?'

'I'll have to see how things go, honey.'

She hung up, and for a moment he was ashamed and unhappy. She was much the same age as Penny Ann.

The Europa Centre was crowded with shoppers, and Miller felt depressed as he stood in the flower shop and waited while they selected the red roses from the tall metal vases on the wet floor. The smiling girl offered each bloom for his inspection and then wrapped the roses carefully. She took the twenty-five Deutchmarks and then noted down the girl's address and his message. They would be delivered by hand, she said, in less than twenty minutes.

He walked slowly to the far end of the Centre and turned into the already open door of the gallery. The paintings on the wall were a mixture of art-deco and pre-Raphaelite girls with sad, dying faces. Kokoshka himself would have approved the spirit, if not the execution.

A balding young man in a blue shirt and jeans came from behind a curtain.

'Ah, yes. Can I help you?'

'I'm looking for Fräulein Lemke.'

The young man pursed his lips in obvious disapproval and pointed gracefully to the curtain.

On the door at the top of the stairs was a typewritten card that said 'Heidi Lemke – Privat'.

He rang the bell and the door opened almost immediately. It was the girl from the club and she frowned as she looked at him. She obviously didn't recognize him.

'I don't do business here.'

'I want to talk to you, Heidi.'

'Who are you?'

'A friend.'

'I don't know you.'

'I've seen you at Club Vogel.'

'I've not seen you.'

'I want to talk to you about Arthur Lowrey.'

Interested and aware, her eyes were on his face.

'Tell me then.' And she stood aside to let him into the room. He was aware out of the corner of his eyes of chintz and frills, and cuddly animals on a pink covered divan. She pointed to a wicker chair and sat down opposite him. Away from the lights and atmosphere of the club, she was just a girl. A pretty girl, immature, girlish and hard at the same time.

'What have you got to tell me?'

'You're in great danger, Heidi.'

'I don't believe you.'

'Somebody else warned you about him didn't they?'

She sat in silence biting her thumb-nail, her eyes on his face.

'What if they did?'

'Didn't you believe him?'

'No.'

'Why not?'

She shrugged. 'Maybe he wants me to stay in Berlin. He likes screwing me.'

'You know that isn't the reason, don't you?'

She shrugged but didn't answer.

'You don't mind that he's conning you?'

'He isn't.'

'I can show you proof that he is.'

'What proof?'

'I'll take you and show you.'

'Show me what?'

He looked at the stubborn girl. He hadn't got time to go on persuading her.

'Have you got a coat, Heidi?'

'Of course I have.'

'Put it on.'

'Who the hell do you think . . . ' and then she saw the snub nose of his pistol. He saw she was about to scream and he grabbed her, his hand across her mouth. He held her tight until she stopped struggling and then said quietly, 'Heidi, I told you that you were in danger. You've got mixed up in something quite by accident. I promise you that you'll be quite safe if you come with me. Do you understand?'

She was trembling violently, and he wondered what he could do to avoid frightening her even more.

'Do you understand what I'm saying, Heidi?'

She jerked her head.

'Will you co-operate with me, Heidi?'

For a moment she hesitated, then she nodded her head. He took his hand from her mouth. Ready to put it back if she went to call out. He noticed a fleck of blood where her teeth had cut her lip.

'Who was the other man who told you about Lowrey?'

She shrugged. 'A cop.'

'What's his name?'

'Schiller. Inspector Schiller.'

'Where's your coat?'

She pointed to a fur coat lying across the foot of the divan. When he helped her on with it, he said, 'You'll be paid for any lost time, Heidi.'

'Where are you taking me?'

'It's not far.'

She sighed and shivered. She knew he wouldn't tell her where they were going. She turned the key in the outer door and then followed him down the narrow stairs.

There were two browsers in the gallery but she walked straight through. He saw the car waiting at the exit to the Centre and opened the rear door for her to get in. He sat beside her as they headed for Leitzenburgerstrasse and the Ku'damm.

The traffic was heavy, and it was half an hour before they pulled up outside the Grunewald safe-house. It was beginning to snow again and the wind drove it into their faces as they walked towards the house.

Briers was waiting in the hall as they went inside.

'Fräulein Lemke. Sunny, will you take her to one of the rooms and see that she gets coffee or a drink.'

'Class one?'

Miller shook his head. 'No, that won't be necessary.'

Miller went to his own room, took off his coat and stood looking out of the window. There were patches of light on the snow shining from the windows, but otherwise it was pitch black as far as he could see. The sky was heavy with snow, and it was piling up like cotton-wool around the window frames.

He needed every morsel of information that he could get about Lowrey, and he needed it fast. The girl was the only source he had, and now he'd got her, he wasn't sure how to tackle her. He wasn't even sure that she knew anything that he didn't already know. If he had had more time he wouldn't have risked involving her merely on the off-chance that she might know something. Both of them, Lowrey and Laufer, were amateurs, petty crooks who didn't have any idea of the size of the bomb that they were holding.

He looked at his watch as he walked down the corridor, it was already past six. He saw Briers come out of the furthest room and signal to him.

'D'you want a guard outside while you're in with her, David?'

'No, thanks.'

The room was bare except for three chairs and a primitive desk, and his heels clattered on the bare boards as he pulled up a chair alongside her. She sat huddled up, still in her coat.

'Would you like a drink, Heidi, a whisky?'

She shook her head.

'How long have you known Lowrey?'

'About eight days.'

'You told Inspector Schiller that Lowrey was trying to blackmail a German politician didn't you?'

She nodded.

'Why did you tell him if Lowrey's your boyfriend?'

'Schiller said he'd check up on him for me.'

'What else did you tell Schiller?'

'The politician's name.'

'What were you going to do in the blackmail scheme?'

'Nothing.'

'Are you in love with Lowrey?'

'He asked me to marry him.'

'What did you say?'

'I said I would.'

'Why?'

She shrugged her shoulders. 'To get out of Berlin. To get British nationality. He said we would be equal partners in a club in London.'

'With the blackmail money?'

'I suppose so.'

'So you *were* in the scheme. You were an accessory.'

'No. I didn't do anything. I just listened.'

'You would have been a receiver.'

'How was I to know where the money came from?'

'Why is Laufer involved in it?'

'Arthur doesn't speak German. And he doesn't know his way around.'

'How much was Laufer getting?'

'Half whatever it was.'

'Who has the letters?'

'Lowrey.'

'Has Laufer got copies?'

'I don't think so.'

'Why don't you think so?'

'I've heard him ask for copies and Arthur's fobbed him off. But Laufer's seen the letters.'

'The originals?'

'I don't know.'

'Where does Lowrey keep the copies?'

'He carries them round with him.'

'All the time?'

'Yes.'

'On his person?'

'Yes, in his jacket pocket.'

'Have they contacted the politician?'

'Yes.'

'Tell me what you know.'

'Laufer's been phoning him, and he went across once to see him.'

'When is he paying them?'

'In the next three days. Laufer phoned him at his office this morning and said they wouldn't wait any longer.'

'What did the man say?'

'He said he'd got most of the money. Would they accept less. Laufer said no. But I think they will. Arthur wants anything he can get.'

'Have they talked about what they would do if he couldn't pay?'

'Yes. They said they'll send the letters to the KGB in East Berlin.'

'Do you think they would?'

'I think they'd only send the copies.'

'But you think they would?'

'I'm sure they would. Laufer's spent a lot of time on this. And it's Arthur's only chance. He'd go berserk if they didn't get the money after all this.'

He looked across at the window, wondering if he could avoid the last question. But he knew he couldn't. It would be leaving a trail for somebody else to follow. Maybe she wouldn't know the answer. He turned to look at her.

'Do you know what's in the letters?'

'The chap was a traitor in the war.'

'What did he do?'

'He worked for the British Gestapo, spying against Germany.'

'Do you think the letters are genuine?'

'They look genuine.'

'You've seen them?'

'Yes. Arthur showed them to me.'

'The originals?'

'No. Just the copies.'

'You never answered my question.'

'What question?'

'Are you in love with Lowrey?'

'He's OK.'

'No more than OK?'

'I guess not.'

'Do you know where he keeps the originals?'

She hesitated only a second but it was enough.

'No.'

'No idea at all?'

'No.'

'It might save his life if you had even a vague idea.'

'I haven't.'

'How long are you going on working at the club?'

'If I'm on my own until I've got enough to start a salon.'

'What kind of salon?'

'A hairdressing salon.'

'How much have you saved?'

'About twenty-five thousand marks.'

'How long did that take?'

'Four years.'

'How old are you?'

'Eighteen.'

'You started at fourteen?'

'Yeah.'

'How much more do you need?'

'The same again.'

He stood up. 'I'll be back in a few minutes.'

He turned the key silently on the outside and slid it into his pocket.

In his own room he used the internal phone to trace Briers.

'Has the money come over yet, Sunny?'

'The dollars have.'

'I'm in my office. Send someone up with ten thousand quickly.'

'Will you sign for it?'

'Sure.'

He waited impatiently until the money came up, clean, and still banded from the bank. He signed the chit and hurried back to the girl, carrying the money sealed in the three big, brown envelopes.

She was standing at the window when he let himself in.

'Sit down, Heidi.'

She walked over slowly, slightly defiantly, as if she regretted what she had told him. He handed her one of the envelopes.

'Open it.'

She opened it carefully and slid out the packets of notes. She pulled one note out to look at the reverse side and then looked back at him.

'What's this for?'

'To help you remember where the originals are.'

'I don't know. I told you.'

'There's ten thousand dollars altogether, Heidi. He must have told you something.'

She stared across at him.

'He said they were somewhere where only he could get

them. Even if someone found out where they were, they couldn't get them without him.'

'Go on.'

'I don't know any more. He didn't like talking about it.'

Instinct told him that she was telling the truth. He gave her the other two envelopes and left her, locking the door behind him.

Briers was waiting for him in his room.

'You'd better transfer the girl to a class one room. Contact Parsons and tell him I want the two snatch teams over here as soon as possible. Are the surveillance teams sending their reports here now?'

'Yes.'

'I'll see their reports and then the teams, in an hour from now.'

'What are you going to do?'

'I'm going to get some sleep. It's going to be a long night, Sunny.'

'Parsons sent some mail over for you.' He pointed to some letters on the pillow.

There was a brief letter from the solicitors informing him that Mrs Miller had instructed them to withdraw the petition for divorce. They also asked in solicitor's mealy-mouthed jargon if they 'could look to him to defray their charges so far incurred'. A letter from the building society informed him that the mortgage interest rate was being increased by $\frac{1}{2}$%. And a note from the Special Forces Club reminded him that his subscription was overdue. Finally there was the letter that Penny had sent to him in the USA to announce that she had left him. He read the first page and the last paragraph and then screwed up the pages and tossed them into the open fireplace. He took off his jacket, shoes and trousers, lay back on the camp-bed and closed his eyes. He wished that the girl had not known the basis for the blackmail attempt.

It was Briers who woke him an hour later.

'They're all here, David. They're waiting for you.'

He washed his face in cold water and brushed his hair. As he looked in the cheap mirror, the face that looked back at him reminded him that he was forty-three on 10 December. He didn't look older, but his face was only saved by the deep tan. The puffiness under his eyes, the deep rifts each side of his nose, and the pronounced muscles at the sides of his mouth bespoke a life of tension. His grey eyes stared back like the eyes of a wary, hunting animal. He dressed slowly. If all went well this would be the last time he would be physically involved in one of these operations and . . . He shook his head irritably to get his mind back to what he was doing.

Briers was waiting for him in the corridor and he followed him down the broad, sweeping staircase to the hall, and through to a large room that had been cleared of its furniture, now only holding rows of chairs, a projection screen and a blackboard. There was a scraping of chairs as a dozen or so men half-stood as Miller walked to the blackboard.

'Good evening, gentlemen. Has anybody not read the descriptions and seen the photos of Laufer and Lowrey?'

Nobody spoke. Miller turned to Briers.

'Where's Lowrey at the moment?'

'At the Pension Allgau.'

'Who are the team leaders?'

Two men sitting together at the end of the first row put up their hands.

'Your name?' Miller pointed at the bald man.

'Speidel.'

'And yours?'

'Townsend.'

'Right, Mr Townsend. Take your team off and pick up Lowrey. If you have to use drugs, use a minimal dose. I need him talking by the time I get back. There's a small chest of drawers at the side of his bed. You should find two letters there. They're photocopies. If they're not in that chest, two of you stay and search the place. Fifteen minutes only. If you

175

don't find them in that time forget it. I want all his belongings to come here. Don't book them in. And don't book *him* in. It's of the utmost importance that you don't cause any public rumpus. Any questions?'

Townsend stood up. 'Is he armed, sir?'

'Not so far as I know. Anything else?'

Townsend shook his head, looked around, and four men left with him. Miller turned back to look at those who were still there.

'Mr Speidel, I want you to pick up Laufer. I'll go with your party. He's going to be more difficult. The club will be starting to fill up so there'll be witnesses. Laufer is probably armed. Dress like customers, pay your way in, take a table. I'll already be in the club. As soon as Laufer goes in his office, I'll go in too. Two of you come in after me. Two stay at the table in case you need to keep things quiet. There's a door from Laufer's office that leads into the hotel next door. You'll take him through there. Bring him straight back here. Don't let him see Lowrey. I'll go back in the club for a few minutes and I'll want a car waiting for me. Again, the minimum of disturbance. You'll all carry your mini-radios. I'll radio back here for someone to phone Laufer as soon as we're all inside. Any questions?'

Speidel didn't stand. 'Can I suggest we use an extra man in police uniform. He can stay in the second car in case he's needed.'

'Good idea. You fix that. Fifteen minutes from now, if that's enough time for you.'

'That's OK, sir.'

'I'll go first. Give me five minutes to settle in.'

Seventeen

The wheels of the BMW spun wildly as they turned out of the gates, and cinders rattled on the chassis as they got onto the forest track. When they reached the highway, they were back in the real world again – a world of neon lights, shops, restaurants, cinemas, cars, and people. People living ordinary lives, who knew nothing of the things that went on in their name. By the time they were on their way back to their houses from their evening out, a lot would have happened. And if he did it the way he had been trained to, they would remember only the film or the meal.

His hand reached again and again inside his jacket for the gun under his left arm. Touching the butt, warm from his body, checking the safety catch, lifting the gun in its chamois leather holster to check that it would slide out freely. The car dropped him about fifty yards from Club Vogel, and he walked back casually towards the entrance. The pianist was playing 'Misty' as the girl took his coat. Laufer himself came welcomingly towards him.

'Glad to see you back, sir. What'll you drink?'

'A Scotch.'

Laufer snapped his fingers to one of the girls and told her to bring a large Scotch.

'Business going well, sir?'

'Fine, thank you. Where's Karen?'

'Just a moment. I'll find her for you.'

He returned immediately. 'It slipped my mind. I've sent her to check on one of the girls. She's not turned up. Karen will be back in about half an hour. How about one of the others while you wait?'

'That's OK. I'll wait for her.'

'She'll be very flattered when I tell her that.'

Miller nodded, and sipped his whisky as Laufer moved away to another table. There were very few people in the club and Miller looked at his watch. Laufer had moved to the door to welcome two Japanese customers. He saw Briers' men at their table, talking to one of the girls. He waited two more minutes, then switched on the tiny radio in his pocket and brought it up to his mouth. He pressed the grey button and said softly, 'Phone.'

It seemed a long time before the phone rang in Laufer's office. Laufer shouted an order to a girl as he walked briskly towards his office. Miller pressed the grey button again, and said, 'Now,' as he stood up. He looked round vaguely as if he were perhaps looking for a toilet, and then he strolled casually towards Laufer's office.

Laufer was bent over his desk jiggling the rest bar up and down on his phone. His back was to the door and he said, *Scheiss,* as he slammed it down. As he turned to head back for the door he saw Miller.

'This is ... ' He stopped as he saw the gun and his hand reached out towards his desk.

'Don't do that, Laufer. Nobody'll come.'

'What the hell's going on?'

'Take off your jacket.'

'Don't be so ... ' He stopped speaking as he saw the two men walk into the office. They stood each side of Miller.

'Take off your jacket. And hand it to me.'

Slowly, Laufer slid his arms out of his jacket and held it out to Miller who took it and shook it carefully. It wasn't heavy enough to be holding a gun. Miller handed it to the man on his left.

'Roll up your trouser legs.'

The knife was taped to Laufer's right leg just above his ankle.

'Turn round.'

Laufer obeyed and the man on Miller's right bent down and peeled off the knife. Miller took Laufer's jacket and put it over the German's shoulders.

'We're going to walk through into the hotel, Laufer, and out into the street. You'll talk about the weather and you'll be smiling. Understood?'

Laufer nodded.

'Get going.'

Miller stood aside and nodded to Speidel who took over. Miller walked to the office door, slid out the key, transferred it to the other side and locked the door behind him as he stood for a moment facing the club-room. He strolled back to his table and sat down. Nobody seemed aware of anything abnormal. A few minutes later he stood up and walked towards the door.

As he was handing over the ticket for his coat, she came in from the street. With snow on her hair and her white raincoat, she looked young and fresh and beautiful.

'Hi, Karen,' he said quietly.

'You're not going already?'

'I'll be back.'

'Was it you who sent the red roses?'

He smiled. 'Why me?'

'Because you're that kind of man.' Her blue eyes caught his and then she kissed him gently. 'Did you see Heidi today?'

'Yes.'

'She hasn't turned up tonight.'

'Maybe she's got a date.'

'Not in working hours. She needs the bread.'

He kissed her cheek. 'See you later, honey.'

'Will you book me for tonight?'

'I'll phone you later.'

'Here?'

'Yes.'

As he came out into the street he saw the brief flash of a car's headlights way down the block. It was snowing again but the wind had dropped. It was Christmas-card snow – soft, heavy flakes that drifted gently down, settling for the night. A gritting lorry was spraying its coarse sand halfway up the sides of the parked cars as it moved slowly along the street.

As he slid into the back seat of the car, he notified the safe-house that he was on his way.

Schiller was still at his office when the call came through on his direct line.

'Schiller.'

'Is that Inspector Schiller?'

'Yes.'

'This is Karen, Inspector, Karen from Club Vogel.'

'What can I do for you?'

'It's Heidi, Inspector. Heidi Lemke. She's gone missing.'

'That's a matter for the city police, fräulein.'

'Herr Laufer is missing too. They had to break into his office. The old man at the hotel said Herr Laufer had left with two men and he looked disturbed. Heidi told me that she'd spoken to you about a personal thing. I wondered if this was anything to do with it.'

'When did she go missing?'

'She left the gallery about four this afternoon.'

'Alone?'

'No.'

'Go on.'

'The man at the gallery says she left with a man.'

'A regular?'

'She doesn't do business at her place.'

'Who were the two men who left with Laufer?'

'Nobody knows. They came into the club as customers.'

'Then what happened?'

'Laufer went into his office to answer the phone. A man followed him in and then the other two.'

'I thought you said Laufer left with only two men.'

'The first man came back in the club again and left a few minutes later.'

'So why did they need to break in the door of Laufer's office if this guy was the last one to come out? Was the key on the inside?'

'No. The key's missing.'

'What made you phone me?'

'I'm scared for Heidi.'

'Come on, sweetheart. It's more than that.'

'I'm frightened for me too,' she said softly.

'Why?'

'The man at the club was one of my clients. He'd been to the club before.'

'Did Heidi tell you what she told me?'

'About the blackmail you mean?'

'Yes.'

'Yes, she told me.'

'Did she tell you the victim's name?'

'No. I don't think she knew it.'

'Tell me about the man.'

'He's mid-forties, maybe even fifty, tall, attractive, very tanned.'

'Any regional accent?'

'He isn't German.'

'For Christ's sake, girl. What is he?'

'I think he's a Yank.'

'Why? Why not English?'

'He's got a kind of American accent.'

'Kind of. What's that mean?'

'He uses American words.'

'Like what?'

'Like "honey" and "guy".'

'Did he tell you his name?'

'David Miller. That's the name he gave. I don't know if it's his real name.'

'They never give you girls their real names. What's he like in bed? Is he normal?'

'Yes.'

'What did he talk about?'

He registered the long pause before she spoke.

'He asked me about Heidi's boyfriend, Arthur Lowrey.'

'Go on.'

'He paid me to find out where he lived.'

'Anything else?'

'He rang me this morning to find out where Heidi lived.'

'What else?'

'Nothing else.'

'OK,' he said slowly. 'If you think of anything else, phone me. I won't forget your call, Karen. If you ever need a helping hand, let me know.'

Schiller reached for the phone and sent one of his men to check Lowrey's room at the Pension Allgau. Then he leaned back in his chair, his hands clasped behind his head as he looked contemplatively at the portrait of Konrad Adenauer on the far wall of his office.

There had been nothing in Lowrey's room that gave any indication of anything out of the ordinary. He went over the things again – toilet stuff, a few tatty bits of underwear and shirts, a couple of letters, a pair of slippers, a few coins in the ash-tray, an old copy of *Playboy* and the carbon slip for the return flight back to London.

He wondered if the letters might be a clue. He neither spoke nor read any language other than German, but although these were only photocopies it had looked as if the original letters were old, the paper yellowed at the edges. They looked official, and government letters weren't likely to provide blackmail material.

He leaned slowly forward, reaching for the telephone, and reluctantly he requested his opposite number in the city police to put out a general call for Lowrey, Laufer and Heidi Lemke.

The signals unit at both safe-houses monitored the instructions to foot-police and car-patrols, and the texts of the messages were passed to Miller.

Eighteen

Lowrey was handcuffed with his hands behind his back, the handcuffs threaded each side of the centre slat in the back of the chair. His jacket was on the trestle table, its contents neatly laid out alongside it. A small heap of coins had a card beside it that read, 'Contents of trouser pockets'.

Miller sorted through the nondescript items: handkerchief, two biros, a Post Office Savings Book showing a balance of £124, a driving licence two weeks out-of-date, a membership card for the Ruby Club, 17a Old Compton Street, and the return flight ticket to London. The photocopies of the two letters were placed apart at the back of the table. The greasy wallet was real leather, its seams open in places where the stitching had disintegrated. A tattered letter from the Midland Bank dated April, 1957, confirmed that his account had been closed. He also found a typed copy of a summons against Lowrey, Arthur, and others, for operating a brothel at the Cobra Club, 97 Lower Wardour Street, and a court receipt for payment of £100 bail together with a routine demand for £34 costs from the Court Administrator at Great Marlborough Street. There was a photograph, cracked along its folds, of a pretty blonde girl in a flowered summer frock, sitting on a rock with the beach and the sea behind her. A straw hat with flowers hung from one hand. She looked like a pretty country girl from an H.E.

Bates short story. There was a postcard-sized photograph of the same girl, naked, coupling with a negro. There were seven pound notes, a ten shilling note, a postal order for nineteen shillings, and thirty-five marks in five-mark notes, a thin pale-blue Bundes Post receipt, a membership card for Club Vogel, a Post Office book of twopenny stamps with four left, a condom in a torn paper packet, and the two joined halves of tickets to the Odeon Leicester Square. The passport was new and apparently genuine. The clothing was grubby and minimal.

Miller reached for a chair and drew it up to sit facing Lowrey. There was a trickle of blood from the corner of his mouth and a bruise on the left side of his face. His washed-out blue eyes looked back at him with venom. Miller realized that Lowrey hadn't recognized him. But there was no real reason why he should.

'Have they charged you yet, Lowrey?'

'For what?'

'For offences under the Official Secrets Act.'

'You must be out of your bloody mind, mister.'

'Why do you say that?'

'What's the Official Secrets Act got to do with me? Anyway we're in Germany.'

'You don't remember me, do you?'

Lowrey stared at him for several moments and then shook his head. 'No. I don't.'

'The two letters are addressed to me.'

He saw the animal eyes narrow.

'What letters?'

'I haven't got much time, Lowrey.'

'For what?'

'To argue with you.'

'That's up to you, squire.'

Miller could feel his patience and control slipping away. After Lowrey and Laufer, he'd still got to go over and get Richter. And sooner or later the West German police would

185

have put the pieces together and black BMWs would be sweeping up the drive of the safe-house to see what was going on.

'Where are the originals, Lowrey?'

Just the start of the sly smile had been enough, and the palm of his hand crashed against Lowrey's face.

'Where are they?'

Lowrey was panting as he looked back at Miller, his eyes moving quickly to find a clue as to what would happen next. He ducked as Miller stood up. Miller grabbed Lowrey's hair and wrenched back his head.

'Where are they, Lowrey?'

'You won't find 'em, you bastard.'

Miller's hand reached down between Lowrey's legs and squeezed, and as Lowrey screamed he squeezed again. Lowrey's face was contorted with pain and he tried to lean forward in the chair but the handcuffs held him upright.

'Where are the letters, Lowrey? I'm in a hurry. You can have more of this. I can go on all night if that's the way you want it.'

Lowrey was groaning, shaking his head as the red-hot pain flowered again and again between his legs.

Miller's hand reached down again and Lowrey cried out, 'For God's sake. I'll tell you. Just leave me alone.'

'Where are they?'

'At the Post Office.'

'Which Post Office?'

'The big one. The main one.'

'Are they in a locker?'

Lowrey looked up at Miller's face. 'I'll sell 'em to you.'

'How much?'

'A thousand quid.'

Miller relaxed and sat down.

'OK. Tell me where they are and what you've been up to.'

'Can I have a drink? Some water?'

'When you've told me what I want to know.'

'I just wanted some dough, that's all.'

'Where are the originals?'

'They're addressed to me at the Post Office.'

Miller remembered the blue Bundes Post ticket.

'Where's the receipt?'

'You've got it. It was in my wallet.'

Lowrey flinched as Miller stood up suddenly and headed for the door. In the passage outside Parsons was standing with Briers.

'What time does the main Post Office close, Sunny?'

'Ten o'clock.'

Miller hurried back into the room, picked up Lowrey's passport and the Bundes Post receipt, and went back to Briers.

'Send a man to the central Post Office. There's a packet there addressed to Arthur Lowrey. Here's the receipt and here's his passport. Get the packet back here soonest, unopened. Have there been any police reports back to Schiller?'

'We haven't heard any.'

Miller turned and hurried back into the room. There was vomit down Lowrey's shirt and his face was white and drawn.

As Miller sat down, he said, 'How many copies did you make?'

'Two.'

'We've got one, where's the other?'

'Are you gonna pay me?'

'Yes, but it'll have to be in US dollars.'

'That's OK.'

Miller saw the relief on Lowrey's face. He really thought he would be paid and released.

'So where's the other copy?'

'In my right shoe.'

Miller bent to unlace the shoe, and there in the sole were

187

the crumpled, stained copies. They were damp, and as he pulled them out they fell apart at the creases. Ignoring the stench, he folded them out and checked them as he walked over to put them on the trestle table.

Back with Lowrey, he said, 'Who else knows about this?'

'Nobody.'

Miller said softly, 'Haven't you had enough? You tell me one more lie and there won't be any warning. I'll finish what I started. Who else knows?'

'A German named Laufer at Club Vogel.'

'Who else?'

'Nobody.'

Miller's fist crashed into Lowrey's face and blood gushed suddenly from his shattered nose.

'Who else, Lowrey?'

'It was just the two of us.'

'Who else did you *tell*?'

'A girl. A German girl, she doesn't know what we were doing.'

'What's her name?'

'Heidi Lemke. She works at the club.'

Miller's hand reached towards Lowrey's crotch and paused. 'Who else did you tell?'

'Nobody. I swear it.' He screamed. 'I'll swear it on the Bible if you want.'

Miller withdrew his hand. 'Did you tell anyone in England?'

'No.'

'What about Joe Cappa?'

Even that battered face showed its surprise.

'D'you know Cappa?'

'Why did you keep those letters in the first place?'

Lowrey sighed heavily and shrugged. 'Jesus. I just wanted something interesting to keep. A souvenir of my job in the war.'

'But why *those* two letters?'

'They were in the same file. One was at the top of the file and one at the bottom. They were the easiest to pull off.'

'Did you keep anything else that should have been shredded?'

'No. It didn't interest me.'

'So why that file? Why that particular day?'

'I was waiting for the shredder to finish the previous batch. I looked at the stuff while I was waiting. I thought it was probably the last shredding job I'd get.'

'Why did you keep them all those years?'

'God knows. I forgot about them. I never looked at them.'

'So why did you look at them now?'

'I saw the German's picture in the paper and recognized him. I remembered the letters. I wasn't even sure I'd still got 'em.'

Miller got up slowly and left the room. The steel door locked automatically behind him. Parsons was standing in the corridor, his hands in his trouser pockets.

'How's it going, David?'

'Where's Briers?'

'In the radio room.'

'I want to talk with you both. Quickly.'

'Let's go downstairs.'

'No. I want to talk in my room.'

Parsons' eyebrows raised for a moment and then settled back. Miller looked tired enough not to be queried on anything he wanted.

Miller sat on the edge of the camp-bed and Parsons and Briers at the card-table, their chairs turned towards him.

'I've interrogated Lowrey. I've got both photocopies. The originals you know about. I'll burn all three sets myself. I'm ninety-nine per cent sure that only Lowrey and Laufer know about Richter in war-time, and I'm a hundred per cent sure that they don't know any more. The girl, Heidi Lemke, wasn't part of the blackmail attempt but she knows what it was based on.

'As I see it, there's no way we can let any of them go. They could always come back for more. They could tell other people, either intentionally or just as gossip. Do you two agree with my view of the situation?'

There was a long silence. Then Parsons spoke. 'What about Richter?'

'I'll go across for him tonight or tomorrow.'

'If you get him back what harm could Lowrey and Laufer do?'

'They can talk, for God's sake. The West Germans would pursue it. The East Germans and the Soviets would pursue it. Once *they* got on the wavelength Richter's life wouldn't be worth a dollar wherever he was.'

Briers shifted on his chair. 'It could take the sting out of the revelations about the Harting woman.'

'Does that matter at this stage?' said Parsons.

Miller was too old a hand to snatch at coat-tails that were trailed as obviously as that.

'That's why I'm consulting you two.'

'What do you think?'

'You know what I think.'

'What?'

'I think the three of them have to be chopped.'

Parsons looked across at Miller. 'D'you want me to consult London?'

'That's up to you. I shan't take umbrage if you do.'

Parsons nodded. 'I'll see who I can raise at this time of night.'

There was a long silence after Parsons had left until Briers said, 'You must feel knackered, David.'

Miller shook his head. 'I can't afford to. There's too much still to do.'

'We'll look after these three.'

'It's going to be difficult with all this bloody snow around. The ground will be as hard as iron. And Schiller and his boys will be round here sooner or later.'

'I can hold him off. I've got plenty on friend Schiller.'

'I'd like to know who tipped him off tonight.'

'All in good time. I'll find out when the dust's settled a bit.'

'What's Laufer doing?'

'Full of fire to start with. Kidnapping, assault, invoking everything he could think of from the United Nations to Amnesty International. He's quiet as a mouse right now.'

Then Parsons came in. Miller noticed that he was smoking a cigarette and that as he took it from his mouth, his hand was shaking.

'London leave it to you, David.'

'Don't bullshit me, Parsons. What did they say?'

Parsons shrugged. 'They agreed with your assessment and your solution.'

'So why are you worried?' He had nearly said 'scared'.

Parsons sighed. 'It's a lot different on the spot from being at a desk in London.'

Miller smiled. 'You chaps always say that a desk gives you a wider perspective.'

'There are other things than wider perspectives.'

'Like what?'

'Like your hand, for instance.'

Miller looked down at his hand. His knuckles were swollen and skinned, and there was dark brown blood over the back of his hand and wrist, and on the cuff of his white shirt. He wondered for a moment if he would get like Parsons after he'd sat behind a desk for a few years.

There was a knock on the door and a man came in with a white envelope, snow still clinging to his black hair. When he had left, Miller opened the envelope and pulled out the two letters. He looked up at Briers.

'Can you get me the two photocopies off the table in there?'

Miller watched the papers burning in the wash-basin, the acrid smoke making his eyes smart. When there was nothing but black ash, he turned on the tap. When there was nothing but a grey sludge, he pulled out the plug and left the tap running until the bowl was clean again.

Nineteen

Miller stood in the shop looking at the three silver spoons. Two were antiques and one was modern. The modern one was plain and functional, and its beauty was in its shape. He put it to one side and gazed again at the two antiques. They were old-fashioned traditional christening spoons. One had a certification that it was a genuine Paul de Lamerie, made for Kaiser Wilhelm. The Imperial arms had been engraved on the curved handle and were just discernible. The other had a heart shaped on the curve of the handle, its original fullness worn smooth from handling. Two ribbons were intertwined along the handle itself, to end in a slightly raised love-knot on the back of the oval bowl. He chose the one with the heart and it was placed in its original leather-and-plush case. The leather case, wrapped in cotton wool, was fitted neatly into a cardboard box with the Henckel trademark on its lid.

A pathway had been cleared in the snow on the pavement and Miller walked to the far end of the Kurfürstendamm, almost to the Gedächtnis Kirche. He waited patiently for the green man on the crossing lights, and as the traffic stopped he walked across, and headed for the Rosenthal Studio-Haus. He saw Parsons turn the grey BMW into Meincke Strasse. He knew what he wanted, the six-place dinner-set in the plain white Thomas design with the gilded edges. Ten minutes later, he carried the weighty box out to the kerb, and a few seconds later the grey BMW drew up alongside him.

They didn't speak much on the way back. Miller was thinking of Penny and Penny Ann. They knew virtually nothing about his life. Apart from any question of security, he could never have told them the truth. Who would want a husband or father who did the things he did. In the early days, he had had nightmares himself. But that had been a long, long time ago. There were no nightmares any more. Whichever side you were on, you knew what you were doing and you knew what would happen if your mind wasn't on the job in hand. The body in the woods, or the river, or the hotel room, would be wearing your clothes.

Miller used to look at the dead faces and wonder about sweethearts and wives, and small girls. He kidded himself that it was to check that the right man had died. The scar on his arm was a constant reminder that looking at dead men's faces and thinking sentimental thoughts could end in you joining them. A quick glance was enough, and the sentimental thoughts were for when you landed at Heathrow. If it was day-time they'd both be there in the white MG, and if it was night it would be just Penny. And as they drove down the M4 he would slowly edge back into the normal world. The world of school-reports, new curtains, starlings in the roof space, leaky cisterns and school concerts with Penny Ann Miller singing 'Pennies from Heaven'.

For the second time Parsons said, 'We're here, David.'

Miller sat eating a couple of beef sandwiches at the card-table. Parsons sat near the window and Briers on the camp-bed.

'Are you ready, Dave?'

'Go ahead.'

'West German passport and visa for you. British passport and visa for you. East German passport for Richter. And West German passport for Richter.'

'Which are genuine?'

'All basic material is genuine. The visas and stamps and embossing were done by Facilities Hamburg. All of them will stand anything except forensic laboratory examination.'

Miller looked at Parsons. 'Did they get the personal radio to Richter?'

'Yes. Yesterday.'

'Has he used it?'

'Just the initial check-out. It was OK.'

'Where's mine?'

Briers held up the small, grey, plastic-cased radio.

'It's been checked. You've got two wavelengths on yours. Signals will cover both, right round the clock. D'you want me to check the Walther?'

'No. I'll do that myself.'

'There's an East German travel pass for each of you but you shouldn't need it. I don't think they're using them now.'

'Any idea where Richter is at the moment?'

'He's at a reception the Czechs are giving for the East Germans at their Embassy. He'll probably have to stay until around midnight.'

'Is he expecting me tonight?'

'He was warned to be ready as from yesterday noon. We didn't tell him more than that.'

Miller wiped his mouth with the back of his hand and turned to look at Parsons. 'Who's in charge of Helmstedt now?'

'Stewart.'

'Has he got the files from when I ran Helmstedt?'

'Of course.'

'That's the way I'll bring him back.'

'Is it safe enough?'

'Maybe not, but there isn't time to arrange anything better. It worked in the old days and there's no reason why it shouldn't work now.'

'It's much tighter now.'

'Tell Stewart I'll be using either Helmut or Karl, whichever one's on duty. If he has anyone else tied up who's better, tell him to respond on my wavelength when I ask what the weather's like. He can spell the name backwards. If he doesn't respond, I'll take it that the others are available.'

'The Americans are going to take you through Charlie. They've got your vital statistics and they're providing the uniform. They'll keep going on the other side until you've changed.'

'What kind of vehicle?'

'A jeep.'

'Jesus. It's freezing outside.'

'It's got a canvas hood.'

'And a log fire?'

Only Briers smiled.

Parsons held out his hand. 'I'll go and rouse Stewart. Best of luck.'

'How long will you keep round-the-clock watch for?'

'Fourteen days. London's orders.'

'I'm flattered.'

Richter stood at the edge of the crowd, an empty champagne glass in his hand. In the centre of the huge room the Czechs were showing how much they cared for their East German comrades. An eight-piece orchestra was playing for the Czech National Dance troupe who were dancing to the *furiant* from Smetana's *The Bartered Bride*.

As he looked at the people on the other side of the room he saw that the Russians, as usual, were sticking together. The Russian officers in their smart uniforms always impressed him. Moscow chose carefully whom they sent to the capitals of their Warsaw Pact allies. The touches of gold and red on their uniform gave them a romantic air that made Richter think of troikas in the snow, and Anna Karenina wrapped in silver-fox furs. He was suddenly conscious of someone standing beside him. He turned and saw that it was Wedekind, his own Minister.

'What do you think of it all, my friend?'

'They are certainly honouring us tonight, Herr Minister. They seldom send the State Dancers to embassies. I heard that the last time was Paris two years ago.'

Wedekind took his arm. 'Let's have a chat. See if we can find somewhere quiet.'

They walked side by side down the long, red-carpeted corridor until finally Wedekind opened one of the big, mahogany doors. 'This looks all right, Otto, let's go in here.'

Richter watched Wedekind settle himself into the leather chair. He was seventy now, an old party faithful who had spent World War II in Russia. He had been awarded an Order of Lenin for his services, first in a Soviet artillery unit and then as a commissar liaising with von Paulus.

'Sit down, Otto.'

As Richter sat down the old man leaned forward and put his empty glass beside his chair. He leaned back, crossing his thin legs. 'Have you got any problems, Otto?'

'You mean the Khrushchev visit?'

'No. I mean personal problems.'

'Not that I know of, Herr Minister. Is it thought that I'm neglecting my duties?'

'Not at all. Not at all,' the old man said soothingly.

'What made you ask, Herr Minister?'

'Why didn't you ever marry, Otto?'

Richter shrugged. 'I never met the right woman, I suppose.'

The old man pursed his lips as he looked at Richter. 'You've had women friends, I know.'

'They'll only wait so long for you to put the ring on.' Richter smiled, but couldn't see where it was all leading.

'There are plenty of young party members who would be delighted to keep a Deputy Minister happy in bed.'

'I know. It's a question of time ... ' He shrugged.

'So who is Karl Laufer, Otto?'

'Who?'

'Karl Laufer.'

'I don't recognize the name.'

'He runs a club, more a brothel, in West Berlin.'

'I haven't been in West Berlin in the last three years, Herr Minister.' Richter was conscious of the quaver in his voice, and the cold seeping again across his chest and shoulders.

'You know, we are none of us perfect. If you want a girl it is best you use one of our own. They tell me our girls are as well-equipped as any others.'

'I'm sure they are.'

'Comrade Chukovsky was worried. Is still worried.'

'About what?'

'The visit to your house by the man Laufer.'

'When was that?'

The old man sniffed. 'Let's not play games, Otto. Tell me what it's all about.'

'I don't remember such a visit, Herr Minister. Maybe I don't know his name. I would need to know more. And maybe Comrade Chukovsky is mistaken or his men are mistaken. I find it disappointing that I am under investigation by a Soviet liaison officer. Especially one with whom I have worked for so long.'

The old man snorted. 'You know better than that, Otto. It's their normal attitude to foreigners. And for these purposes we are foreigners too. I'll arrange for you to talk to him and clear the matter up once and for all.' He paused. 'What are you doing about Slanski's wife?'

'I've warned her. I did it myself.'

'You think she'll behave?'

'I've told her that if she doesn't behave they will both be posted to Jeddah.'

'No drink, no women for her, and no girls for him. Maybe we should do that anyway.'

'Would you like me to get you a drink, Herr Minister?'

'No. You'd better get on your way. I'll tell Chukovsky to phone you for an appointment.' He smiled. 'Insist on protocol. Your office, not his.'

'Yes, Herr Minister.'

He stood up, bowed slightly, and headed for the door. In the corridor he walked slowly as the ground seemed to move and sway under his feet like a rope bridge across a river. At the first small passage, he turned and leaned against the wall, resting his head against his arm. He breathed deeply and drops of sweat ran from his face down under his chin to his chest. Slowly, he stood upright and looked around. There was nobody there, watching. He walked heavy-footed to the end of the passage, turned and walked back, trying desperately to regain his composure. As he turned into the corridor, the chandeliers seemed to flash and swing above his head and he made his way carefully out of the building to the car-park. He found his car and the sleeping driver who drove him home.

He looked at his watch. It was barely eleven o'clock.

Richter's hand was still trembling as he put the key in the lock and turned it. The cleaning woman had left the light on in the hall as usual, and he hung up his coat and hat on the old-fashioned hall-stand. The place reeked of floor-polish and hot radiators. With one hand on the banisters he hesitated, turned, and walked back through to the sitting room. He needed a whisky and a moment or two to collect his thoughts.

He switched on the lights and walked over to the corner cupboard where he kept his drink. Pouring himself almost half a glass, he turned and held it to the light. It was a malt, his favourite, Glen Grant, a gift from his opposite number in Prague. He sipped it carefully and then took a good mouthful before walking over to the settee and the high-backed armchairs.

He sat down and leaned forward to put his glass on the coffee table. It was then that he saw Chukovsky sitting in one of the armchairs facing him. He looked amused at the shock on the German's face.

'Good evening, Comrade Deputy Minister. I hope I didn't startle you.'

Richter sat paralysed, the same cold spreading again across his chest, his body rigid, his mouth opening and closing as he tried to speak. From far away he heard his own voice saying, 'This is an outrage, Chukovsky. Explain yourself.'

Chukovsky smiled. 'A social visit an outrage? Since when, my friend?'

Richter's hand went up to his neck to loosen his tie, and then, compelled to some action to relieve his tension he stood up clumsily and walked across to the telephone. Chukovsky sat watching him, and as Richter's finger probed for the dial, Chukovsky said, 'Don't waste your time, Herr Becker, your telephone isn't functioning.'

Richter dialled the number twice but nothing happened. He only heard a hissing silence. He turned to look at the Russian. 'I shall report your intrusion to the Council tomorrow, Comrade Chukovsky. You would be well advised to leave now.'

'Sit down, Becker.'

'I must insist that you leave at once.'

'I can arrest you if you prefer that. I thought perhaps that wouldn't be necessary.'

'What is it you want?'

Chukovsky shrugged. 'To talk, my friend. To clear up a small problem.'

'What problem is that?'

'Sit down, Herr Becker.' Chukovsky pointed to the settee.

Richter sat down facing the Russian who lit a cigarette and leaned forward, his eyes on Richter's face.

'Why did the man Laufer visit you?'

'I don't remember such a man, I have already explained that to Minister Wedekind. He is quite satisfied with what I told him.'

'And what did you tell him?'

'That I don't remember such a man.' Richter spread his hands. 'Strangers visit me frequently. Asking for help or advice. Maybe this man was one of those.'

Chukovsky said softly, 'In the last three months you have had only ten visitors. One was from Globus Insurance. He called three times. You took out an insurance on your household goods. You had two men who you interviewed as part-time gardeners. You had three visits from the same girl from Café Tanz. She stayed the night each time. You had a visit from the owner of Briefmarken Lukas and you bought three first-day covers of the Graf Zeppelin South American flight. You paid Michel Catalog less fifteen per cent. And you had your visit from Herr Laufer who runs a brothel called Club Vogel in West Berlin.'

'And what was the purpose of Herr Laufer's visit, Comrade Chukovsky?'

'That's what I am asking you.'

'I've told you I don't remember such a man. Maybe he called here but I don't recall him.'

'You let him out yourself, and he waved to you from the street gate.'

'Who authorized you to carry out surveillance on an East German Deputy Minister?'

'Don't be naïve, Becker. Your department has carried out surveillance on scores of your officials on our orders.'

'We'll see what the Council of State has to say, comrade.'

'I imagine they will merely wonder, as I do, why you don't

just settle the matter by telling us why you had a meeting with a West German pimp.'

'Or maybe they'll think that you have fabricated some story to discredit me and the security services.'

Chukovsky's eyes showed his anger and impatience. 'Or maybe I'll have Herr Laufer brought over and find out what really is going on.'

'What do *you* think is going on?'

'Maybe you want a girl from him. In that case you can forget it, and so can I. Or maybe you're playing more dangerous games.'

'Like what?'

'Who knows? That's what I want to find out.' Chukovsky stood up. 'And that's what I'm *going* to find out.'

Richter stood up too. 'Meantime I shall put a guard on this house.'

Chukovsky smiled. 'He'll be company for my man. I'll let myself out. If you want to talk further with me I'm always at your disposal, Herr Deputy Minister.' He walked into the hall and Richter heard the door slam behind him. The adrenalin pumping through his veins gave him the energy to hurry upstairs and pack a small case. He looked around the bedroom trying to think of what he might have missed, but he knew it was pointless. Everything had to be abandoned before the guard was put on the house.

He walked two blocks and then hailed a taxi which dropped him at Marx-Engels Platz. Ten minutes later he gave the code rings on the door-bell of the bookshop in Unter den Linden.

The two Volkspolizei and the plain-clothes KGB man watched the jeep thread its way through the barriers of Check-point Charlie. Several times a day and twice in the night the Americans and the British asserted their legal right to unhindered access to the East Zone of Berlin. All Berlin, West and East, was ruled by the Four Allied powers. That was how it began in 1945 and that was how it would be until a Peace Treaty was signed.

Apart from the deliberate enforcement of their mutual rights, the military were not provocative. The Berlin airlift and the workers' uprising against the Soviets in East Berlin had made their several points with Moscow. And the grim Wall had given the West Moscow's dusty answer. For all concerned it was better to play for a draw in Berlin rather than risk direct confrontation. Both sides made short journeys into the other's territory and returned peacefully.

Miller sat on the front seat next to the driver, his white helmet, a size too small, clamped uncomfortably on his head. It was a measurement nobody had thought to take. They turned left for Otto-Grotewohlstrasse and by the time they were passing the old bunker Miller had stripped off the bulky uniform and slid his arms into his coat. He searched frantically for his documents, found them in the coat pocket and sorted them quickly to distribute them around his clothes. For a few seconds he closed his eyes and went through a mental check-list. He opened his eyes as his hand slid inside his jacket to check for the Walther. The jeep slowed down as it turned at the Brandenburger Tor and automatically he sprang out. Suddenly he was standing alone, the jeep's red tail-lights far away up Unter den Linden.

He walked up the avenue, crossed the bridge and walked through to Alexander Platz, then left again to Rathausstrasse. He stood in the shadow of a telephone kiosk as a police car cruised by. He took a bus in Grunerstrasse up to the inner ring road and walked towards Richter's house. At the corner of the street he gave Richter's call sign on his radio. There was no response, and Miller stopped and pulled out the fine wire aerial. He called Richter twice more with the aerial in different positions but there was still no reply. He collapsed the aerial and slid the radio back into his pocket.

Turning up his coat collar, he walked slowly down Richter's street. There was a light on upstairs in the house and as he drew level he saw the man standing inside the garden gate. He wore a long leather coat and a black hat with a broad brim. Miller nodded to him with a *'Guten Abend'* as he walked by. The man didn't respond. Miller was sure that he was KGB not Volkspolizei. There had been lights on in a downstairs room but no signs of police activity, and there were no police cars parked in the street. He walked on through to Prenzlauerallee and half an hour later he was at the top of Unter den Linden. The girl answered the door at the bookshop and held his arm as she closed the door.

'There is a friend already here. He's very scared. I think maybe he's ill as well.'

'What kind of ill?'

'I don't know. His face has no blood.'

'When did he come?'

'About an hour ago.'

'Did he use the code?'

'Yes.'

'Is your father worried?'

'Worried. Not scared.'

For a moment he leaned against the wall, his eyes closed as he tried to think. It was beginning to go wrong too soon. The time he needed was being squeezed already. He had known that he would have to improvise, but his options were being sliced away too early in the game. He had not expected that Richter would be under pressure even before they started. He took a deep breath and opened his eyes to look up the steep stairs. He signalled to the girl to lead the way.

In the sitting-room the old man was seated at the table, cataloguing a pile of books, a cigar in one hand, a pen in the other. He looked up at Miller. 'I've put him in my bedroom. He's asleep. I should leave him for a bit.'

'What happened to make him come here?'

'I don't know. I didn't ask. He's in a state of shock. Take off your coat, my friend. Have you eaten?'

'Thank you, yes. Have you got a room I could use for ten minutes?'

The old man pointed. 'My daughter's bedroom.'

Miller sighed, and hesitated before he spoke. 'I need to use my radio. Will you allow that?'

'You mean am I afraid?'

'Maybe for your daughter.'

The old man turned back his sleeve and Miller saw the blue-green, concentration-camp number tattooed on the old man's arm. When he looked at his face he saw the grim smile.

'Yes, I'm afraid. But not afraid enough. You go ahead.'

Miller closed the bedroom door, sat on the bed, and set up the small radio and then pressed the call button. They responded immediately with the code-word and Miller spoke in French as they had agreed. 'Passenger under pressure. No details yet. What news regarding friends southwards?'

'Impossible use that facility. No longer operating. Find alternative and inform us soonest. Out.'

'Understood. Out.'

He looked round the small room as he pushed down the aerial. It was sparsely furnished except for a Klimt print on the wall. One of his pre-Raphaelite beauties, hair streaming in the wind, her eyes closed as she looked up at the sun. He walked back into the sitting-room where the girl was sitting at the table with the old man, reading out the details of the books as he wrote. He realized that he had been stupid to go along so easily with London's insistence on getting Richter out in a matter of hours. If he had had a week or ten days it could have been properly planned with a trained team.

'How long can we stay?'

The old man looked up. 'How long do you need?'

'I'm not sure until I've spoken to our friend. Maybe two days. It depends on what's happened.'

'So stay two days. You can sleep in my daughter's room.'

'That's not necessary. I'll sleep here when you've finished. I'll get us away as soon as I can.'

'Don't worry, my boy.'

Walter Müller sat uneasily and uncomfortably on the concrete slab and looked around the cell. The walls were white-washed, and there was no window. The only light came from a square of thick glass in the ceiling which was covered with a metal mesh that cast a surrealist pattern on the walls and floor.

So many people had told him never to have anything to do with the police. The police meant trouble for any citizen in the German Democratic Republic. In the Wehrmacht days people had always said – never volunteer for anything. And now he had been crazy enough to combine both stupidities at the same time. He had volunteered information to the police, and he had ended up sitting in a police cell at Werderstrasse.

It was nearly midnight when a key turned in the door and the inspector beckoned to him. The effect of the drink was beginning to wear off, but he still needed to put out a steadying hand from time to time, as he walked down the corridor. When he was shown into the brightly-lit office he had to close his eyes for a moment before he headed for the chair.

The police inspector stood at one end of the rough table as Müller faced a white-haired man whose deeply lined face and grey eyes had an air of unmistakable authority.

'Your name?'

'Müller. Walter Müller.'

'Your address?'

'Flat twenty-nine, Münchenburgerstrasse number forty-seven. By the S-Bahn station.'

'Occupation?'

'Electrician.'

'Place of employment?'

'The hospital.'

'Which hospital?'

'The one in Gross Hamburgerstrasse.'

'Tell me what you told the inspector.'

'I saw the American patrol jeep. It slowed down and a man got off.'

'Did the jeep stop?'

'No, it just slowed, and he kind of slid out.'

'What did he look like?'

'Big chap. Broad shoulders.'

'What about his face?'

'I didn't see that. I wasn't that interested.'

'What was he wearing?'

'An overcoat and a hat.'

'What colour coat?'

'Darkish.'

'Why were you there?'

'I'd been to the pub. I was walking back to the station.'

'How much did you drink?'

'Five or six glasses.'

'What drink?'

Müller laughed. 'Beer, mister. Working men can't afford more.'

'Were you drunk at the time?'

'Who knows. I wasn't sober let's say.'

'How often do you go to the pub?'

'Once a week. On pay night.'

'Why didn't you report what you saw straight away?'

'Never came in my mind. I don't know what those patrols are supposed to do.'

'What changed your mind?'

'I told the missus. She told me to tell the cops.' He nodded towards the inspector. 'He told me to come in and see him. So I did. And now I'm in a bloody cell like a criminal.'

'What time did you see this?'

'God knows. Eight-thirty, maybe nine.'

'Was the man young, old or what?'

'Middle-aged. Fortyish, but he was quick on his feet for a big man. Athletic sort of fellow.'

'Was he carrying anything?'

Müller closed his eyes tightly and then shook his head as he opened them.

'I don't remember.'

'When he got off the jeep what did he do?'

'Walked up Unter den Linden.'

'Did he look around at all?'

'No.'

'Where did you go?'

'The same way, he turned into Alexander Platz, and I went on up to the station.'

'Which one?'

'Alexander Platz.'

'You're sure he was dressed as a civilian?'

'Quite sure.'

'How was the driver dressed?'

'American army uniform. White helmet with MP on the front.'

'How do you know it was American not British?'

'Painted on in white. US Army Patrol. And the Stars and Stripes on the back.'

'Was the jeep open or covered?'

'Covered.'

'What kind of cover?'

'Canvas with a plastic window in the side. Same as they always use.'

'Where did the jeep go?'

'Up Unter den Linden.'

'How far up?'

'No idea. I didn't look.'

'Right, Herr Müller. A police car will take you home and I thank you for your assistance.'

'I did right, did I?'

'You did more than that. You were a vigilant citizen, and your wife is a very sensible woman. Good-night to you.'

Lieutenant-Colonel Andrew Kowalski, United States Army, thrust away the hand on his shoulder and turned impatiently in his sleep but the hand went on jogging him until he turned reluctantly, and sat up, still half-asleep.

'Jesus Christ. What is it?'

'Captain Hargreaves, sir. I'm duty officer.'

'What the hell d'you want?'

'The Soviet liaison officer is here. He insists on seeing you.'

'What time is it?'

'Four twenty-five, sir.'

'For God's sake. Tell the stupid oaf to come back in office hours.'

'I tried to put him off, Colonel, but he wouldn't have it. He insists.'

Kowalski sat up, rubbing the heels of his hands into his eyes. 'What's the bastard want?' he said, without looking up.

'Wants to lodge an official complaint from the Soviet Kommandatura.'

'What about?'

'He wouldn't say. Seemed very up-tight and formal.'

'Where is he?'

'In your office. Sergeant Farne's with him.'

'Tell him I'll be down in fifteen minutes.'

'Yes, sir.'

Kowalski washed and shaved, and then dressed carefully. There was a mild gamesmanship that entered the meetings with Soviet liaison officers. Protocol and the courtesies were generally slightly exaggerated.

He walked slowly downstairs and along the corridor to his office. He nodded dismissal to the Marine sergeant and only looked at the Russian when he had settled himself behind his desk. The Russian was a major with the insignia of an artillery regiment, his high cheek-bones indicating one of the eastern Republics. He was in his thirties, and he stood to attention, his cap under his arm, waiting for Kowalski to start the ritual.

'You wanted to see me, major.'

'I am instructed to deliver a note from General of the Army Ostovsky.'

Kowalski held out his hand. The Russian reached in his pocket and brought out a buff-coloured envelope sealed at the flap with red wax. Kowalski put it down in front of him on the desk and went through the next step of the ritual.

'Thank you, major.'

'I am instructed to await your reply, and, if necessary, discuss the matter with you.'

Kowalski nodded and picked up the envelope. 'Sit down, major.' He nodded to the seat in front of his desk. Kowalski used a gilt letter opener and he leaned forward as he unfolded the stiff paper. He read the letter twice, his face impassive. Then he looked across at the Russian.

'You don't expect me to accept this, do you?'

'It is from the general himself.'

Kowalski tossed the note across his desk. It slid to the edge, hung for a moment, and then fluttered to the carpet.

'I don't believe that. The general's got more sense.'

'I assure you that ... '

Kowalski interrupted. 'What exactly is the complaint. You say a United States soldier got down from a patrol jeep. So what?'

'That is against our agreement.'

'You give the general my compliments and ask him to let me know which clause in the Potsdam Agreement prevents

210

any United States' soldier having access, on foot or otherwise, to any part of the city of Berlin.'

'It is an abuse of the permission that is given for US patrols to appear in East Berlin.'

Kowalski's face looked angry. 'We require no *permission* to send our patrols into any part of Berlin. It is a right. A right we exercise every day.'

'East Berlin is controlled by the government of the German Democratic Republic.'

'You know well enough that we don't recognize such a government as having rights in Berlin. The whole of Berlin, so far as we are concerned, and the Potsdam Agreement is concerned, is under the control of the United States, Great Britain, the Soviet Union and France.' Kowalski leaned forward aggressively. 'Your people chose to build a wall. The Wall has never kept us out and it never will. You've been told that before, on three occasions.' Kowalski stabbed his thick fingers on the desk top to mark his words. 'And you are skating on thin ice, my friend. You make one move to hinder our patrols and it will not be you and me. It will be Washington and Moscow. On the red phone.'

The Russian sat calmly. It was what he had been briefed to expect.

'We allow your patrols through Check-point Charlie without harassment or checking on the understanding that they are simply patrols. If they are to be used by civilians that would be a different matter.'

'Who said this man was a civilian?'

'The witness who saw him.'

'How did he know he was not a soldier in civilian clothes?'

'We expect that US servicemen on patrols will be in uniform.'

Kowalski stood up. 'Go back to your friends in Pankow, Major. Tell them it didn't happen, and if it had happened they still would have no grounds for complaint.'

The Russian stood up too. 'I have to tell you, Colonel, that it is possible that we may require to see identity cards of patrols in future.'

Kowalski said frostily, 'I didn't hear what you said, my friend.'

The Soviet officer stood to attention and then walked out. Kowalski pressed his finger on the bell on his desk for a full ten seconds until Captain Hargreaves hurried in.

'Check who was in command of this evening's jeep patrol. I want him here quickly. Was the recorder working?'

'Yes, sir. And I've already checked on the patrol commander. He's on leave. He flew out from Tempelhof to Frankfurt at eleven hundred hours.'

'OK, find me the driver.'

'All personnel on that patrol flew to Frankfurt, sir. On the same plane.'

Kowalski's tongue explored the corner of his mouth and then he said quietly, 'Give General Hopwood my compliments and ask if I can see him straight away. And tell the duty GII officer to stand by.'

'Yes, sir.'

Parsons sat facing Briers, his head in his hands, his fingers combing through his hair. He looked up, red-eyed and sallow-faced, at the younger man. 'What the hell do we do, Sunny?'

'I suggest you consult London. They have to decide priorities at this level, not us.'

'Let's go over it one last time.'

'OK. There's only one way out, and that's through the Wall. Every security man and cop in the GDR is looking for Richter. London want Richter out for a whole raft of reasons. The Americans want Richter out. Our lot *and* the Americans want him out to expose the Harting woman. The Americans won't play again on a patrol jeep. Our people won't play on a patrol jeep. Richter's too ill to come through

212

with false papers on Check-point Charlie. That's about it, chief.'

'We could put together our own patrol jeep and go in and get him.'

'Which *him*? There's only room for one.'

'Miller would have to make his own way back.'

'He'd never make it.'

'He could go to ground and come out when the dust has settled a bit.'

'With no safe-house, and no funds?'

'He's an experienced field officer.'

'Oh for Christ's sake, Parsons, he doesn't stand a chance. They'll be doing house to house checks.'

Parsons leaned back in his chair. 'You're right. Clear the radio room and get me London on the scrambler.'

Briers stood guard himself outside the radio room and ten minutes later Parsons came out. They walked back together to the room that Miller had been using. Parsons sat down and waved Briers to the other chair. Briers noticed a muscle working under the other man's jaw and realized that he was avoiding looking at him. Parsons sat with his elbows on the table, his hands clasping and unclasping as he sat silently with his own thoughts. It was several minutes before he spoke, and his eyes still avoided Briers. 'London insist that Richter is brought out.'

'And Miller?'

'Just Richter.'

'Miller will have one hell of a time trying to get out. And if they get him they'll put him through the wringer. He's bound to talk. He's probably of more real value to them than Richter.'

'London knows that as well as we do.'

'Maybe we could risk a second jeep run the next day.'

Parsons shook his head. 'They're going to announce Richter's crossing as soon as we get him over. Khrushchev arrives in East Berlin in two days time. They insist we get

Richter tomorrow. The Russians are bound to crack down on all the check-points, and London's orders are that neither the Americans nor we are to send patrols through for forty-eight hours, so that the dust can settle a bit.'

'Who do you want on the jeep party?'

'Just you and me.'

'There's generally four.'

'London insisted. Just you and me.'

'I'd better start fixing things. When do you want to do it?'

'Tomorrow night. About eight o'clock.'

Miller had let Richter sleep for a couple of hours before he shook him awake. The older man seemed to be coming up from the depths of the earth as he tried to bring his mind into the present. His pale blue eyes looked at Miller for a long time. Miller sat silently, waiting. Almost ten minutes went by before he spoke. 'What happened, Erich?'

'They saw Laufer come to my house. The Minister tackled me. Chukovsky ignored him and threatened to arrest me. He's putting his men onto watching my house. They've been watching me for months. He knew about Laufer's visit. He knew who he was.'

'Did he know why he came?'

'No, I'm sure he didn't. If he knew that he'd have had me arrested, or just taken to Moscow. That's what he wanted to know. Why did Laufer go to see me?'

'What did you tell him?'

'Nothing. I said I couldn't remember Laufer.'

'Did he believe you?'

'No. When he left I'm sure he would be contacting Moscow for permission to pick me up and fly me out.'

'How do you feel?'

'Very old. Very weak.'

'Do you know if you have anything physically wrong with you?'

214

Richter sighed deeply, and looked up at Miller's face. 'I'm scared, David, and worn out.'

'Did anyone follow you here?'

'I don't think so.'

'Did you check?'

Richter shook his head and there were tears in his eyes. Miller stood up. 'Go back to sleep, Erich. I'll get you out all right. Don't worry.'

'Are you sure you can do it?'

Miller smiled. 'Never lost a patient yet, Erich. What time did you leave your house?'

'I don't remember, David. It's a bit like a dream.'

'Don't worry. Just sleep.'

Miller had written out the message for the old man to code. It was too complex to cover in clear back to the safe-house. The East Germans would have their D-F vans all over the city, listening for any strange radio traffic. And speaking in clear, if Parsons could work it out, the monitoring teams would be able to work it out too. It would be like trying to outline the plot of *Hamlet* without mentioning any names. But this would have to be the only radio contact with London. They'd never break the code but they could pin down the transmission site if there was more than one transmission.

He knew there must be other safe-houses or contacts in East Berlin that SIS controlled, and that was all he could expect: an address, a name, a password and for London to work out some rough code he could use back to Parsons. The old man would have to drop out of the SIS network for at least a year and he'd take his radio and dump it for him. That and the code pads were all that could incriminate him.

It was already dawn when the Pole sat down to transmit. He had tapped out the message onto the tape at slow speed and then timed it at fifteen inches per second. It took two minutes and four seconds. Miller watched as the old man transmitted the call sign. It was naïve but effective. Just three letters repeated three times. DDR. The initial letters of *Deutsche Demokratische Republik*. The response signal came back immediately, the old man pressed down the key and as the counter came up to mark 124 seconds he switched off tape and radio on the main control panel.

Miller packed the radio into its metal case, wound down the filament aerial and put it in the lid of the case. It looked like the usual case that held a workman's tools. He walked over to the window and looked out. It was still pitch black outside and snowing steadily. He looked at his watch. It was 6 am. He noticed the date, 10 December. It had some significance but he couldn't recall what it was.

He let himself out of the shop and looked around quickly. There were no watchers or loiterers that he could see and his were the only footprints in the snow in front of the shop. He joined the queue for tickets at the S-bahn station at Marx-Engels and travelled down six stations to Schoneweide and left the case between two grit containers on the up platform.

The shop was open when he got back. The bell rang as he pushed open the door and turned into the book-lined room. The old man came out from his curtained-off hide-away in the far corner and Miller stood talking to him for a few moments before going back towards the door and the flight of stairs.

Upstairs he lay back in the armchair and was asleep in minutes. He slept until mid-day when he washed and shaved. Just after four, the old man brought up a middle-aged woman, the courier from Parsons. He listened carefully, and asked a few questions, some of which she couldn't answer. She went down into the shop after they had finished and bought a second-hand translation of *Oliver Twist*.

He now had a new address, but they were limited to using it for a maximum of ten days. London wanted Richter over as soon as possible and Parsons hoped to use a patrol jeep.

Code-names for people and places had been provided for 'in clear' radio traffic. Contacts inside the Volkspolizei indicated that Richter's disappearance was already known. There had been no official hint so far that it might be a defection but every part of the police and security apparatus was being used to find the fugitive. There were strong indications that Moscow was venting its displeasure in every direction. The Khrushchev visit was almost certainly postponed or cancelled, Chukovsky had been recalled and there was an unconfirmed report from a contact at the airport that there were bruises all over his face. The comrades in Moscow never minded people seeing what happened to those who failed in their duties. A special team from the KGB had been flown in overnight and had taken charge of the search within minutes of arriving. Everybody who had had even the most distant dealings with Richter was being interrogated in a specially guarded block in Potsdam. Two men, subsequently identified as KGB hit men, had been to Club Vogel, obviously hoping to be able to pick Laufer up and take him over to the other side. They had been picked up themselves by one of Briers' teams as they were queuing at the check-point at Prinzenstrasse. They had not yet 'responded' to interrogation.

It had all sounded cut and dried and well under control but Miller had been on both sides of this sort of operation too many times not to recognize the signs. London wanted Richter out, and quickly. Miller was Parsons' responsibility and Parsons was stuck. He hadn't enough experience and Miller knew what he would have to do. Once Richter was over he would make his own way back. Nobody had really explored the northern coast as a way out. It would be hopeless for civilians but with an RAF chopper or a Royal Navy Vosper it could be a different story.

It was a backstreet of ramshackle buildings, garages converted into workshops and storage facilities. On one side of the passage was a place where furniture could be repaired and, on the other, the board advertised a glazing service. They walked up it until over the arched doorway Miller saw the painted sign. 'Max Baumann. Auto Reperatur'. There was a small door let into the main wooden door and it swung open easily. He held it open for Richter and as he stepped inside himself a young man came towards them. In his thirties, short and stocky, his grey eyes looked at them both with suspicion.

Miller held out his hand but the man ignored it and Miller said softly, '*Wer ist in Himmel.*'

The man replied, '*Vater unser*,' and held out his hand.

He took them to a small office at the far end of the workshop. In the corner was an ex-Wehrmacht camp-bed with a grey blanket. The rest of the furnishings were wooden boxes. On the wall was the standard colour print of Lenin and a portrait of Rosa Luxemburg torn from a magazine.

Max Baumann wasn't a talker, and he asked no questions. He showed them around, asked them not to go into the workshop area without checking first that nobody was there, and then went back to working on a motor-cycle.

During his radio contact with Parsons at five o'clock, Miller had listened carefully to the instructions. As he wound in the aerial he realized that they were leaving him to make his own way out. They hadn't said so but that was implicit in the instructions. After the jeep had picked up Richter he was to let Parsons know his plan and London could lay on whatever facilities he needed. There was no sense of urgency. But maybe that was their tribute to his self-sufficiency. And maybe not.

The forty-watt bulb hung from the wire that had been trailed over one of the rusty metal beams in the workshop roof. Over the two oil-stained benches a long strip of peg-board held an array of small tools and cardboard packs of fuses, wires and small parts. At the edge of the circle of dim light stood a small car with the bonnet removed to give access to its engine. Behind the car were two ancient motor-cycles, one with its rear wheel missing. The dark blue van stood with its radiator almost touching the garage door as Max Baumann tested its lights.

Richter sat on an upturned wooden box covered with a newspaper, and Miller, in a boiler suit, leaned against the work-bench, smoking. He looked again at his watch. There was another ten minutes before they needed to start. The timing had to be accurate because it would arouse suspicion if the van was parked for longer than a few minutes. Miller guessed that they had picked the open space in front of the Brandenburger Tor because it was generally deserted except in the summer, when the crowds listened to the bands that played in the evenings.

The snow was thawing, and when Miller had checked that afternoon there was only a thin layer of dirty, grey slush in the streets. It would make driving tricky but there would be little traffic on the side-roads at night. Miller looked over at Richter. He sat with his eyes closed, at the end of his tether. Like Parsons he was an administrator not a field operator. He was used to giving orders that led to violence and death, but he had never been part of it. He wasn't a coward, no more than was Parsons, but he had had neither training nor experience in the field. He was worn out with fear. He would know all too well the net that the KGB and the Sicherheits-polizei would be throwing round them. He must have organized such networks himself many times. Every metre of the frontier under double watch and, in Berlin, the check-points crowded with watchers with orders to stop him – with a bullet if necessary. If they got him alive, it would be the military plane to Moscow and long weeks in the Lubyanka as they beat his soft flesh to a pulp until he'd gone over every day of his life from school to the day he was caught. Richter had had a kind of courage in the days at the RVPS and even more to cross over from the West to the East all those years ago. But the courage to face brutality was a different kind of courage, the kind that Richter didn't have.

At that moment the light on the small radio in the palm of Miller's hand glowed red. He pressed the button and put it close to his ear. The voice seemed far away as it said the two words three times that meant that the jeep had just passed the Gedächtnis Kirche.

He tapped Richter on the shoulder and as he opened his eyes he signalled to him to stand. Miller turned and flashed his torch to the far end of the workshop and Baumann walked out of the shadows and took Richter's place on the box. Miller bound his arms and legs with the oily rope and finally stuffed a wad of cheese-cloth into his mouth. He planned to come back and release him before he headed up towards the Baltic, but in the unlikely event that he was caught before he got back Baumann had his story to tell of how he was set upon and tied up.

He helped Richter into the passenger seat, opened the garage door and drove the van down the narrow passage. Just before the street, he stopped the van and walked back to close the garage door. As he did so he realized why the date had seemed significant. It was his birthday.

It was beginning to rain as he turned into Weinertstrasse and by the time they were in Prenzlauerallee the wipers were barely coping with the mud thrown up by passing vehicles. He almost crossed on a red light at Spandaustrasse as his eyes strained to see through the dirty windscreen. He glanced quickly at his watch. The jeep was due at Pariser Platz in three minutes. He drove slowly into Otto Grote-wohlstrasse and saw the jeep heading towards the Branden-burger Tor. He turned quickly behind it, followed as it circled the big island in the middle of the square, and pulled up behind it as it stopped on the far side.

Richter clambered hurriedly down and Miller ran with him. He stood aside as Richter clambered in, fleetingly aware that the driver was Sunny Briers. The other man reached across the seats and he saw to his surprise that it was Parsons, rain on his face and his grey hair soaking wet. His glasses were pushed up onto his forehead, and there were golden reflections from the street lights in the raindrops on the lenses.

Only at the last moment did he see the gun in Parsons' hand as a street light glinted on the fat silencer. He was opening his mouth to speak when the first shot smashed between his eyes. The second shot took him in the chest and flung him backwards. He made no sound, and he lay there on the wet road on his back as the jeep sped off, its rear wheels spinning as they fought for traction on the smooth wet tarmac.

The world's greatest thriller writers now available in Panther Books

Len Deighton

Twinkle, Twinkle, Little Spy	£1.95	☐
Yesterday's Spy	£1.95	☐
Spy Story	£1.95	☐
Horse Under Water	£1.95	☐
Billion Dollar Brain	£1.95	☐
The Ipcress File	£1.95	☐
An Expensive Place to Die	£1.50	☐
Declarations of War	£1.95	☐
SS-GB	£1.95	☐
XPD	£2.50	☐
Bomber	£2.50	☐
Fighter (non-fiction)	£2.50	☐
Blitzkrieg (non-fiction)	£1.95	☐
Funeral in Berlin	£1.95	☐
Goodbye Mickey Mouse	£2.50	☐
Berlin Game	£1.95	☐

Ted Allbeury

Snowball	£1.50	☐
A Choice of Enemies	£1.95	☐
The Special Collection	£1.95	☐
The Only Good German	£1.50	☐
Moscow Quadrille	£1.95	☐
The Man With the President's Mind	£1.50	☐
The Lantern Network	£1.50	☐
The Reaper	£1.95	☐
Consequence of Fear	£1.50	☐
The Twentieth Day of January	£1.50	☐
The Alpha List	£1.95	☐
Palomino Blonde	£1.95	☐
The Other Side of Silence	£1.95	☐
Codeword Cromwell	£1.95	☐
The Lonely Margins	£1.50	☐
The Secret Whispers	£1.50	☐
Shadow of Shadows	£1.95	☐
All our Tomorrows	£1.95	☐
Pay Any Price	£1.95	☐
The Girl from Addis	£1.95	☐

All these books are available at your local bookshop or newsagent, or can be ordered direct from the publisher.

To order direct from the publisher just tick the titles you want and fill in the form below.

Name _____

Address _____

Send to:
Panther Cash Sales
PO Box 11, Falmouth, Cornwall TR10 9EN.

Please enclose remittance to the value of the cover price plus:

UK 45p for the first book, 20p for the second book plus 14p per copy for each additional book ordered to a maximum charge of £1.63.

BFPO and Eire 45p for the first book, 20p for the second book plus 14p per copy for the next 7 books, thereafter 8p per book.

Overseas 75p for the first book and 21p for each additional book.

Panther Books reserve the right to show new retail prices on covers, which may differ from those previously advertised in the text or elsewhere.